D'Arcy

by

Donna Doe Southall

DORRANCE PUBLISHING CO., INC.
PITTSBURGH, PENNSYLVANIA 15222

ISBN # 0-8059-6539-4
Printed in the United States of America

First Printing

For information or to order additional books, please write:
Dorrance Publishing Co., Inc.
701 Smithfield Street
Third Floor
Pittsburgh, Pennsylvania 15222
U.S.A.
1-800-788-7654
Or visit our web site and on-line catalog at www.dorrancepublishing.com

To my children:

Christopher Lee Southall (Kit)

Mary Clare Southall

Kirby Donaldson Southall, M.D.

Paulette Ann Southall Weiss (Polly)

Contents

Introduction

"Is it true?"
"Why did you write it?"
"How long is it?"

Every year my sixth grade class asked these questions as I began to read *D'Arcy* to prepare for our annual overnight class trip to Jamestown and Williamsburg. For thirteen years I accompanied my Stenwood students from Vienna, Virginia.

The plot moves on actual historical events from 1619 to 1622. Now for the real persons whose stories are as close to historical fact as I could tell them are: Governor George and Lady Temperance Yeardley; Governor Francis Wyatt; John and Jane Rolfe with her parents, Captain William and Jane Pierce; the Reverend Richard Buck; the Reverend Richard Bolton; the Burgess Roger Smith; John Pountiss; Secretary John Pory; Sergeant Fortesque; and the Indians: Chanco, Debedeavon, and the Old Chief Opechancanough.

D'Arcy began as the result of a creative writing assignment. After the class trip of 1968, I asked the class to choose a partner and imagine how they would fit into life at early Jamestown. "You write one too," they challenged. The next day they read their stories and asked for mine. Their only comment was, "Then what happened?"

Every day I would go home, brew a pot of tea, and write a new chapter. What logically would happen next? The following year the class begged for more. "Aren't you going to tell about...?" The dramatic and far-reaching events that emerged were shaping the history of Virginia and of the United States of America. The book was completed in 1969.

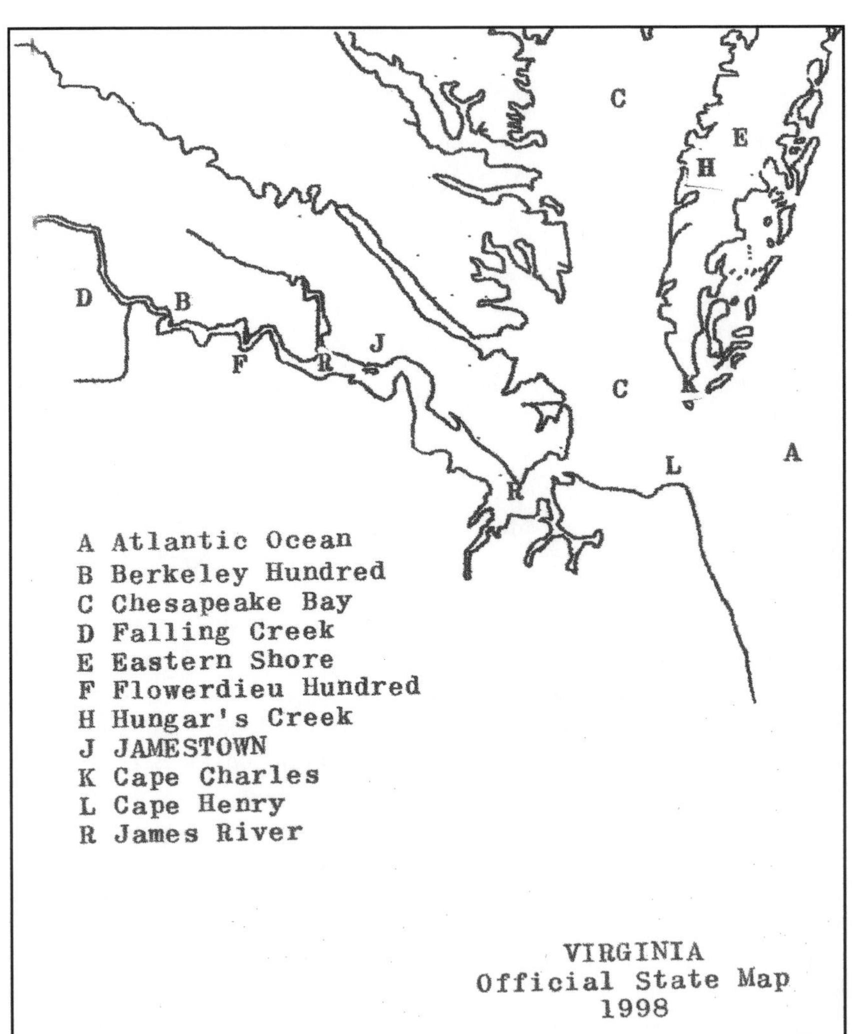
C
E
H
D
B
J
F
R
C
K
A
L
R
A Atlantic Ocean
B Berkeley Hundred
C Chesapeake Bay
D Falling Creek
E Eastern Shore
F Flowerdieu Hundred
H Hungar's Creek
J JAMESTOWN
K Cape Charles
L Cape Henry
R James River
VIRGINIA
Official State Map
1998

The Stocks

Locked in the stocks.

"How long?" D'Arcy asked with a scowl twisting his usually handsome face.

"Three hours it is for sleeping at divine service."

"Even on one's day of arrival?" D'Arcy asked, looking at the guardsman with half-lowered eyelids.

"It matters little. Not that it is my place to say, but more respect ye should have been showin' for our Reverend Buck. And him all the while thankin' the Lord for your safe voyage! Now when I came over the waters, it was a miracle indeed that our ship lived through the storm and the mountainous seas that were churned up. Nobody slept when we thanked the Almighty for bringin' us safe into shore, I can tell ye!"

What was there to say?

Back to the church strode the guardsman to watch for other evildoers. D'Arcy shifted to ease the discomfort already beginning. This narrow edge of a plank made a miserable seat. He supposed that his legs would tingle before long from lack of circulation.

Stocks were a simple but fiendish contraption. His legs, stretching out in front of him, were resting over the edge of a second plank. Half circles had been cut out to keep his legs in place. Another plank, with matching half-circle cutouts, had been lowered and locked in position. Being a little taller than others, D'Arcy looked at his poor feet dangling farther beyond the holes than the average man's would have done. Mercifully his hands were free. He could push down on the board edge where he sat to ease his weight a little. Had the guardsman failed to tie his hands behind his back as a small gesture of kindness?

It seemed a long time before the church service would be over. Then he would at least have some diversion in watching the people who would henceforth be his fellow townsmen. To keep his mind off his growing discomfort, he thought of his excitement earlier in the day when, aboard the sea-weary ship, he had made ready to debark at Jamestown. He recalled all that had happened to bring him to this predicament.

England Lies Astern

As the shores of Chesapeake Bay were slipping by only hours ago, D'Arcy had been thinking how much he would welcome going ashore. His young body yearned for action! He looked forward to exploring the shore, to become vigorous after these weeks of cramped, idle life on shipboard. Eagerly he anticipated having sufficient water to soak himself and his clothes. Ah, to be clean again! He sensed the shiver of excitement throughout the ship as she veered to port to enter the mouth of the broad James River. Hours later came the shout, "Jamestown Fort in sight to starboard."

Crowding the ship's rail, the passengers relished this moment so long awaited during the tedious weeks at sea. The Jamestown settlement was slowly emerging from the misty, wooded shoreline. The ship, free at last of the ocean swell, rode smoothly up the river under cloud-drifting skies. It was one of those days surprisingly warm for February in the year 1619.

D'Arcy's shoulder leaned against the rail as he peered forward at the ship's prow slicing through the brown water. His eyes swept across the broad river. On either shore, as far as he could see, were woodlands rolling away to the horizon. Ahead lay Jamestown, growing ever larger.

Never had he imagined, even in his conversations with the captain and crew, that the fort would look so small. The triangular shape stood out sharply against the forested background because its palisade had been recently replaced, and the sharp-pointed logs looked raw and unweathered. The flag of England rode proudly on the afternoon wind. Now he could make out the tiny figures of men on duty at the upraised gun positions on two of the three visible angles of the fort. How far they had come to see this sight!

The ship had crossed the Atlantic by the usual route—from Plymouth on a southwesterly course to the West Indies. After taking on fresh water and supplies, they had sailed northward up the Virginia coast. Once the Spanish settlements in northern Florida had slipped below the horizon, they had seen no white men's settlements along this low-lying seacoast.

With the Englishman's inborn fascination with mystery, the whole ship's company tried to catch a glimpse of the site of Sir Walter Raleigh's colony at Roanoke. Why had it vanished? Some said it was wiped out by some illness. Others said the Spanish were jealous of another nation challenging their century-long progress in planting colonies. The captain's authoritative voice rose, and they fell silent. He maintained that it was a swift and sudden Indian attack that wiped out the homesites and took the people captive. The Indians would have been too curious about the newcomers to kill them. He told how Governor John White had returned to England for more people and supplies, but Queen Elizabeth would not let him have either, so desperate was her need to offset the challenge in 1588 of the Spanish Armada. After the Spanish fleet had perished in battle and storm, the governor had come back to find that his colony had vanished. No, not even the men who were climbing the rigging could see a trace of the neglected colony.

Now D'Arcy shifted his position and longed to stand upright. When had this headache begun? When he was watching the bee in church? If only he had a drink of water! Desperately he set himself a question to ponder. What was the greatest threat to Jamestown? The Spanish?

How crippling to Spanish power in the New World had been the defeat of the Spanish Armada? D'Arcy knew all available English ships had fought that fleet as it sailed into English waters. He knew a hurricane had blown the ships still afloat up and around Scotland and Ireland, where most had been shipwrecked. Was King James right in thinking that Spain was now too weak to prevent him from founding English settlements? Their very lives depended on the answer.

Oh, his shoes seemed heavy as lead at the end of his numb legs! Indians. Think about them for awhile.

The Indians must realize that if they were to stop this taking over of their lands, it must be soon. They must see ship after ship bringing more settlers and supplies. They could see new settlements springing up along the James River. He had overheard talk on the ship of a mighty Indian chief, Powhatan, who had united some thirty-five villages in a confederation.

An icy finger of fear raced along D'Arcy's spine as he considered how many warriors this Powhatan had the power to gather whenever he wished to do so. It would be bows and arrows against guns and cannon, but the Indians would have untold numbers of men to oppose the scattered colonists. What were they waiting for?

His pounding headache made him think of illness as a threat to his people. There was talk of fevers and a strange malady they called the bloody flux that came on suddenly and caused death in a day or two.

Grinding his teeth, he wondered, "When will I get released from this hateful thing? Well, here is my first challenge. It is up to God if I am to meet with failure or success in the dangers and adventures that lie ahead."

In wretched discomfort, he raised his eyes to the pines, tossing and sighing between river and fort. They were like no English trees. A rising breeze brought him their scent, and its strangeness shot him through with a pang of homesickness. This would not do! It must be this headache. Think of the landing.

Earlier this afternoon, he recalled, he had been part of the confusion of docking and landing. Then the pale sandy soil, littered with broken oyster shells, crunched under his heavy leather shoes. The motion of the ship had still been in his legs. He had paused, hitched his sea chest to a more comfortable place on his shoulder, and moved on toward the gate of the fort. He wondered when he would be getting the rest of his belongings that had been stowed below decks. Fellow passengers had surged past him. He was in no mood to talk. This was too great a moment to share. He had reached Virginia! Up the path and through the gate. He returned a word of greeting to a man with, "Yes, from Southall, near London."

With several other men, he was assigned a wattle and daub hut, where he chose a corner and sank down upon his sea chest. He looked at the interwoven gray branches of the hut walls with the thin spatter of dried plaster that partly covered the branches. That was all the protection there was from rain and wind and sun. Did it ever snow? The roof was thatched with thick bundles of coarse reeds, which overhung the walls by a wide margin as good protection from heavy rains and hot sun. The huts were quite like those of the lower class at home, and he would get used to them in time.

Then a surge of excitement had brought him to his feet as curiosity replaced his momentary nostalgia. What is the fort like? What weapons do we have? We? He smiled as he realized he was already thinking of himself as one of the townsmen. Above the cackle of hens in a nearby pen, there was the high-pitched, excited talk and laughter as the settlers exchanged news with new arrivals. There was the hurry and bustle as more passengers and badly-needed supplies came into the fort. The people of the fort continued to greet those still coming in and begged for more news of affairs in England.

D'Arcy squirmed now from remorse as well as from his nearly unendurable aches. His legs were asleep, but his arms and shoulders ached from the strain of trying to change position. "Remember how you broke their law, merited their punishment, and disgraced yourself on your first day among these people," he reflected.

A bell had tolled, causing the sounds and activities suddenly to change. The townsmen, calling to the newcomers to join them, drew near the church. On entering they arranged themselves in the accepted order: first Governor Samuel Argall with his council sat in front on benches that had backs. Behind them the men sat on simple benches, while the few women stood along the rear wall. The clergyman, Reverend Richard Buck, took his place at the upper of two pulpits and conducted the service. It was full of thankful prayers for the new strength in men and supplies, now safely arrived.

D'Arcy had found a seat toward the rear as he felt befitted a newcomer. The voice flowed on and on from the pulpit. The heat from the assembled people mounted. A huge bee hummed by, and he thought about that early spring bee and how it could leave when it liked. He caught up his head with a jerk as he fought drowsiness and a dull feeling in his head. He fixed his mind on the words, "and in His bountiful mercy, amid the heathen souls of this virgin land…"

A sharp rap on the head brought him instantly around. He looked up into the red and angry face of a guardsman, who gestured with his staff for D'Arcy to follow him. As he rose to his feet, D'Arcy looked at that staff and thought how unfair it was to hit a sleeping man with such a cudgel. By the time he was fully awake, he had been locked in these stocks. Now at long last, church was over.

The women openly giggled and whispered behind their hands as they passed him by. Men shouted with laughter and hurled insults at him. A couple of tough-looking boys, who had undoubtedly had experience in these stocks, tossed a handful of pebbles at him. One clipped him in the forehead. "Dirty!" he raged inwardly. "Hitting a fellow pegged down like this! It is swelling up too, worst luck, but it missed my eye."

The people were moving toward the tables set for the evening meal. Pangs of hunger added to his assorted miseries. The smell of roasting meat, the sweet fragrance of cornbread, and the hearty scent of boiling beans came his way in waves that had earlier excited him, but now he found them not at all appealing. The happy sounds of people eating their evening meal began to ebb. The clanking of pots and cutlery finally ceased. Shame, pain, and homesickness swept through him. How much longer? His throbbing head bowed in utter misery.

"Learned yer lesson yet, have ye?"

"Yes, sir, surely."

"Enough for yer first offense, seein' that but today y'arrived." As the cruel bar was raised, D'Arcy's numb legs were ablaze with pain as he lowered them to the ground and after awhile rose slowly to his feet. He stumbled to the hut where he had left his chest. Drawing out his blanket, he threw himself onto the bare ground and drew the blanket about him. Sleep came within minutes to release him from the agonies of his landing day.

The Flux

A cock crowed. Birds twittered in a variety of sounds that were new to him. Somewhere one hammered rapidly on a hollow tree. Others called stridently as they flew past his hut. A goat bleated.

D'Arcy rolled over on the unyielding ground and tried to find more warmth in his blanket to shut out the damp chills seeping across the cold dirt floor. His head felt thick and dizzy. With growing consciousness, he realized his throat ached and felt parched. His stomach was shot through with griping pains that could not be simple hunger. By the time people were rising and heeding the bell to worship, he was feverish and moaning from time to time. As he had not appeared voluntarily, a guardsman came to fetch him to the service.

Jerked to his feet, D'Arcy reeled outside. This motion caused the worst nausea he had ever experienced. Bolting from the scene, the guardsman went to report that this new man had the flux. D'Arcy thereby got a reprieve from attending church and from the daily work assignment. Staggering into his hut, he sank down, pulled the blanket about him, and found comfort in sleep.

A fellow ship's passenger dropped by after church. When he saw D'Arcy's flushed face, he rushed away to bring him a gourd of cool water and a little food, should he want it. The water brought temporary relief, but all that day his tortured stomach could not tolerate even that for long. For two days he could keep down only some of the tea that he found out later was made from sassafras roots. This hot drink gave him not only relief but lifted his spirits. Yet even more welcome was the lad Jamie, who brought it. His was the freckled face, D'Arcy realized, that had been near when the fever lessened at times and permitted him to remember where he was.

On the following morning, he rose with the others in his hut to take part in the activity around him. He went to the first community meal since he had arrived. Bits of the conversation began to interest him.

"Feelin' better are ye? I didn't ever expect to see ye sittin' at table, breakin' the Lord's bread."

"Amen to that," said another. "Two of yer shipmates failed to pull through this sickness we call the bloody flux, and we buried them at sunup. You are fortunate to be alive."

The first continued, "You'll be havin' yer own prayers o' thanksgivin', come meetin' time shortly. Picked a fine day to rejoin us, so you did. Most of the day we'll be sittin' in prayer meetin'. Three hours this morn it is and then two more after the midday repast. This is the reason we have the break in our fast early on the Sabbath."

D'Arcy slowly munched another piece of cornbread and drank of the fresh goat's milk. How humble he felt to be alive this beautiful morning! In his heart he thanked God for aiding him in his struggle from the nightmare of illness and to be on the way to regaining his vigor. "Who were the men who died?" be asked when he could trust himself to speak.

"I do believe they said the first one was Jones and the other was called Bradshaw."

"Not Dick Bradshaw gone!" D'Arcy gasped. This had been a shipboard friendship that had enlightened the months-long passage. "I'll commend his soul to…." Suddenly D'Arcy rose and departed, lest the men think him unmanly.

To dry his tears and to strengthen his fever-weakened legs, he walked about the fort. He must build up his strength for that lengthy service! The backless bench would be a blessing compared with the tormenting stocks, but he must not fail again.

The sun felt warm on his skin. He felt his health returning as he drew in deep breaths of the piney air. He looked at the cannon and at the guards on the three rounded angles of the fort. How much of an assault can we withstand, he wondered. The fort, the small group of men, and whatever armament they could muster seemed pitifully small and ineffectual pitted against the Spanish and the Indians in this endless wilderness. Yet a beginning had been made, and nobody had yet challenged their right to be there.

As the bell began to toll, he picked up a small pebble and put it in his mouth. This would help to ward off unbearable thirst. Lagging to the rear of the gathering throng, he took a seat nearer the door in order to get more fresh air this time. He managed well enough, and eventually the first session ended. A light meal was set out to refresh the congregation, after which the second session would begin.

A man sought out D'Arcy and said, "Enough meat for the evening meal is not yet brought in. Would you forego your attendance at prayers to join me in the hunt?"

"I will gladly attend you, sir!" Perhaps this reply had been a bit too hearty, for several bystanders were putting on Sabbath frowns.

Leaving the fort they went down to the river and set the sail in a small boat. Presently they heard the church bell pealing across the water. It was D'Arcy who sighted a large buck, which the hunter dropped with a single shot. Together they loaded the kill into the boat, then went on upriver. They took a doe beside a small stream and returned to Jamestown to help prepare the meat for the cooks.

By now the people were walking around, stretching cramped muscles and aching backs. As the shadows lengthened, D'Arcy stood by the fire where the venison was roasting. The baking cornbread sent out little steamy puffs of mouth-watering fragrance. Here was promise of hearty, satisfying food. How hungry he was!

"Ho, Jamie," he hailed the lad who had befriended him. "I am greatly indebted to you for your care these past days."

"'Twas but a squaring of accounts, sir," Jamie replied with an elfin smile. "To my last day I'll be rememberin' the words o' comfort ye gave me when we first put out to sea, and me awishin' I'd never gone a'tall, what with the way I was missin' m' home and m' family."

"I have been well repaid," said D'Arcy, moved by the boy's words. "You have now become a cook's helper, and I must not detain you at a busy hour. We shall talk later."

That evening D'Arcy feasted well on the bread and the meat procured through his own effort. At last he had experienced a good day. The need for sleep came suddenly upon him, so he retired before dark to his hut.

The good Jamie had brought straw and had stuffed the canvas ticking, which D'Arcy had taken from his sea chest with the plan to fill it himself that evening. It was good to lie down on such a comfortable bed. The blanket felt soft and warm. How his family would scoff at his finding any satisfaction in such commonplace accoutrements! With this amusing thought, he fell asleep.

The Brick Toter

Cock's crow came before he thought it possible, but D'Arcy felt refreshed. For the first time since his arrival, he awoke with a feeling of strength and purpose.

Today after church he was told to join a work party, which was building a house in New Towne. With the fort area becoming overgrown, houses of brick were appearing among these of wattle and daub. A handsome site it was with a fair view of the James. Down the center of the town ran a wide street with narrow lanes running from it between the home sites. Some householders already had fences to protect garden plots and wells from roving animals.

A breeze lifted the new foliage. The smell of new plant life was very noticeable to D'Arcy after all those weeks at sea.

The making of bricks at Jamestown in 1612 had been a great undertaking, and one that had developed steadily. Now D'Arcy was to carry some of these bricks to the bricklayers, or masons as they were called. These bricks were a source of civic pride. Fine bricks of fair weight.

Within the hour, so it seemed to D'Arcy, the bricks had doubled their weight. In the next hour their very size seemed to double. As they grew, so did the blisters on his hands. Still they grew, wrenching muscles that had never before done this sort of manual labor. Increasing fatigue in the mounting heat of the day could end only in disaster.

Dickin's Tale

That night, over their tankards of ale, men were still laughing and retelling the tale to those who had not yet heard it. Then there was hearty laughter all over again. The mistakes of newcomers were hilariously funny to those who had so recently acquired the knack of survival.

"Tell Jamie how it happened, Dickin, do! Right from the first now like you been tellin' the others. Start with..."

"Then let him do the tellin', Tom."

Dickin, brushing the back of his rough hand across his mouth, began his tale again. "Well, Jamie, ye ken the young man D'Arcy Southall? A younger son, I'd say, from some fine family. Near London maybe from his talk. The day the ship dropped anchor, he went to sleep in church, he did. Got himself fixed up nice and comfy in the stocks for it."

"A fine welcome that," added Tom, "for a young gentleman who was expectin' the paths here to be shinin' wi' gold. And all of us townsmen dancin' in the streets, he'd expect, because he had come to join us!"

As the laughter ebbed, Dickin went on, "Nobody even thought to give him a bite to eat that night when he was released from the stocks. What with the excitement of the ship comin' and all. He must have gone straightaway off to bed."

"Not very sociable of us, would you say?" asked Tom.

"A welcome like that and Dickin here," announced the storyteller jabbing his thick thumb at his chest, "would ha' evermore kept all his best yarns to himself." And he beamed at his listeners who were moaning and exclaiming in mock dismay.

"Just missin' the evenin' meal would have finished me."

"We know that, Jamie."

"Well, the next morn," resumed Dickin, "as with several of the other new arrivals, he woke up sick with the bloody flux—the bloody flux itself."

"Must ha' been comin' on him when he fell asleep in the church," said Tom.

"All them hours in the stocks and no supper neither, poor lad," someone muttered.

"Might ha' been the missin' o' the meal that saved 'is life," stated another.

"Are you sayin'" piped up a furious Jamie, "that it was some o' *our* cookin' that led to those burials of the newcomers these past few mornin's"?

"No-o, but in my opinion it is better for a man to be fastin' than feedin' when that sickness takes him. Since nobody knows much about the cause or the cure, however, one opinion is as good as another."

"Do get on with the story, Dickin."

"Well, the first mornin' he's up, he is faced with goin' to services or goin' to the stocks if he misses. And what day would this be but Sunday with our five hours of church." Here the men had to smile at the humor of the situation, but it did not seem right to laugh, considering the religious nature of the subject.

"Now the hunter," went on Dickin, "took pity on him at midday, and asked him to help fetch deer for the cooks. This brought him around so well that he was put on a work party next morn."

"Not totin' bricks!"

"Totin' bricks it was. Of course, he had never in all his life before done work like that. From the start that was plain enough. You should ha' seen him by late afternoon! Fair totterin' he was."

"Now comes the best part. Tell us, Dickin."

"Up onto the platform he carried his bricks to Will and John, who were layin' up the bricks with mortar, you see. They were buildin' a wall to the new buildin'. Up he'd tote his load, then down he'd go for yet another. Up and down, up and down he went. Then came the trip when his weary foot did not qui-te make the top step. Headlong he tripped!

"Now the bricks, fallin' forward as they were, toppled Will against the new wall. And the wall, with its new mortar not yet hardened, of course, collapsed! What with tryin' to get out of the way, John kicked over the mortar bucket. So there you have all in a scramble, the wall fallin' down, the three men thrashin' about, and the spillin' mortar-r-r!"

When the shouts of laughter subsided, Dickin went on, "You would think it was bad enough for the day's work all gone for naught, but who do you suppose, Jamie lad, was watchin' all this from first to last? None other than Governor Argall himself!" Here Jamie's elfin face showed such wide-eyed shock that even the storyteller himself joined in the whoops of rollicking laughter.

"The governor ordered them to set about savin' the bricks right away. All three fell to scrapin' off the mortar before it hardened fairly in the hot sun. Save them they did, but three more disgusted men you would not be findin' in all the New Wor-r-rld!"

"Will D'Arcy Southall go back to brick work?"

"That will he not. The governor made it quite clear that on the morrow he is to go out with a fisherman."

Fishing and a Talk with Jamie

Rodney Gale and D'Arcy between them were carrying a basket of fish to the cooks. The rockfish, trout, bass, and flounder had been cleaned, ready to be cooked, and D'Arcy was thoroughly tired of them. What rotten luck!

All day he had been learning what was involved to procure the river fish that made up a sizable portion of the colony's diet. He had found what a struggle it was to manage the stubborn skiff on the choppy waters. He had helped Gale to drag in the heavy, wet nets, empty them, and reset them without getting them entangled. Together they had hauled up the fish traps that acted reluctant enough to come out of the water, but then threatened to blow away on the strong gusts of wind. And this wind had chilled and chapped his wet hands until they ached.

Even after they had moored the skiff, their job was not done. There was still the job that D'Arcy found loathsome and altogether endless: cleaning the catch. There were several species that required scraping off the scales as well as gutting. His world was full of the odor of fish. His clothes were wet and cold from the spray and soaking gear, and they were spattered with the sticky, smelly, silvery scales of the slimy creatures. His hands hurt even more from the awkward way he had grasped the fish while cleaning them.

However he had tried to hold the fish at first, the sharp fin tips would pierce his long-wet hands. By watching Gale out of the corner of his eye, he finally saw how he should hold the slippery thing. He would try sliding his hand down from the head.

There were few words exchanged. In fact, D'Arcy looked as if he had forgotten how to smile, while Gale's mouth was set in a straight, grim line. It had been like this since D'Arcy had lost the largest netful of fish. Just as they were about to empty this fine catch, the merciless wind had healed the skiff over, and the rail on D'Arcy's side suddenly dipped almost to the water line. To save himself from pitching overboard, he had instinctively let go of the net, frantically clutching the rail while Rodney Gale roared his protests, and the fish slipped away in a gleaming surge to freedom.

The weary men lugged their basket to the cooks. Jamie watched his chief cook peer inside and lift an eyebrow. Jamie knew the cook was thinking of all the hungry people who would have to be satisfied. Jamie was watching D'Arcy's face when the cook asked, "Is that all?"

D'Arcy felt his heart go heavy inside him like a cold rock. Something pushed up so hard that it made his throat and jaws ache. He was cold, wet, tired, hungry, and he stank of fish. He went to his hut to peel off his wet clothing. He pulled on something dry, took some soap with his wet garments, and strode off with long strides to a nearby stream.

For a long time he scrubbed himself and his reeking clothes until he felt clean. As he rinsed the last of the things in the cold running water, he sensed his self-esteem returning. On bushes he spread his laundry to dry in the afternoon sun. Then he sank down on a log and let his head rest on a handy tree. His hands looked red and damp and revoltingly wrinkled.

It was the first time that he realized he was proud of his hands. They were well formed and looked capable.

What can I use them for in this miserable place? If that is my attitude, I shall give it all up and go back. No. I do not want to give up. What is needed is work what excites me because I would use my own talents. I was well trained to use an active mind and body, but never to toil as a common laborer. No wonder I have been a failure! What can I do that others here cannot? What can I contribute to the colony's present needs...and perhaps to its future development? Either I have too little ambition or overmuch!

He gave a long sigh and watched an odd blue and white bird move headfirst down a tree trunk. Suddenly he smiled as a thought struck him. In this land it might be necessary to take off in an entirely new direction! Just then came the sound of approaching footsteps.

"There y' are, Mr. Southall. Ye washed y' clothes."

"Yes, Jamie, I am not used to smelling like a fish monger. Come and share my log."

"My family was used to keepin' clean too, and my mum worked hard washin' up for all o' us."

"How many in your family?" asked D'Arcy, more to keep the talk going than from any real interest.

"Ten when ye count the parents."

"Do you ever expect to hear from them?"

"No, for none of us had the chance to learn how to read or write, one bein' like the other, I suppose." A silence fell as they thought about this.

"If we wrote to them," now D'Arcy's voice had more interest, "could they find somebody to read the message to them?"

"Why, I wonder if the vicar…yes surely the vicar…there would be one who could read a letter from me. But who…*we* did ye say? Oh, *you!* You know the magic of writin' words down."

D'Arcy laughed at the boy's excitement and at the idea of literacy being magic. To the illiterate, of course, there would be something mysterious in being able to codify one's thoughts so they could be read by another in a different place or even in a different time. He had never thought of writing and reading in this light. "Jamie, we'll send them a letter. You can tell your family of your sea voyage and of your life here in Jamestown. It will make them happy to hear that you are well and how useful…."

D'Arcy left his thought unfinished on a painful subject. Yes, little Jamie had found a place here as a cook's helper and was proving to be a good one. But he, D'Arcy, had yet to earn the reputation of being useful. Bungler—even a laughing stock of the town with his awkward bumbling. Where did he fit in?

As D'Arcy retreated into a world of his own, and a none too cheerful one, it appeared, Jamie quietly studied his friend. He liked the way D'Arcy's blue eyes made him feel important and the smile that showed to advantage his strong, even teeth. His chin, nose, and brow were all well formed. It was a face that Jamie could imagine framed in a knight's helmet, the visor up, as a mounted group set off on a crusade.

It was not a common thing, Jamie knew, for a member of the upper class to befriend one of the lower class. It was the unusual events encountered in settling a new land that had thrown them together in ways where each had had occasion to benefit the other. He would never call this friend by his given name, for that would be taking a liberty that his station in life denied him. It was enough that this man was showing him such kindness.

"After our meager meal," D'Arcy said bitterly as he thought of the small catch, "we shall begin that letter. I'll take these garments back to the hut to finish drying. Are you hungry tonight for fish?" Laughing, D'Arcy ducked away from Jamie's well-aimed pine cone. Together they collected the damp clothing.

D'Arcy asked, "Why did you come to Virginia?"

"Because there were so many of us. My father sent me over as an indentured servant, and I am to work for seven years with the chief cook. Then I shall be a free man and can own land."

"My reasons for coming are not unlike yours. Although my father has wealth, my oldest brother will inherit his fortune, his lands, and even Southall Manor. That is a handsome little seat southwest of London. The law of primogeniture is hard on younger sons in a family, but it keeps the lands and wealth from being endlessly divided as the old people pass on, you understand. Had I stayed on in England, I had a number of choices open to me.

"In the army or navy I could easily have been set up with a commission, for my father has friends in high places. An uncle could have found an appointment for me in the Church of England. I could have been apprenticed to some merchant or to a craftsman to learn a business or trade. But I wanted a new way of life and to see more of the world. With hard work and good fortune I hope some day to own land and acquire wealth. Someday we may both be landholders, Jamie, as we could never have been in all probability back in England."

The evening meal proved ample after all. The hunters had brought in rabbits, which were served up in a stew. Some roots D'Arcy could not yet name were savory and filling, boiled and dressed with a bit of pork fat. The fish were delicious broiled on boards, set close to the fires, Indian-style. Life was far more pleasant with a good supper over, and with the prospects of beginning Jamie's letter.

Then came a sudden change in the weather when wind and a slash of rain drove them all indoors. Jamie joined D'Arcy in the church, where many had taken shelter. They talked of things they would write about the colony and their new way of life. The rain came in a downpour as lightning lit their world in yellow-green flashes. The thunder crashed and reverberated across the river. The chilly night came early.

The Pitch and Tar Swamp

It was with a lighter spirit and more willing hands that D'Arcy took part in the next day's activity. The church service over, the men broke their fast on bean soup, hot cornbread, and gourds of fresh goat's milk. D'Arcy's name was called with those needed in the Pitch and Tar Swamp, a low part of the island that extended toward Back River.

A shipload of naval stores was being collected. In England there would be a growing demand for the products of American woodlands: tall timber, pitch, and tar. The tall pines were needed for the huge masts and the long timbers required for the larger ships that were under construction. These larger ships would be used for the distant trade with the Far East, especially India, as well as increasing voyages to America to found more colonies. Pitch was used to make the hulls seaworthy, as it was smeared where two timbers were joined. Tar was needed to make the ropes and lines water-resistant and so extend the life of their usefulness. This cordage was an all-important part of the rigging, and the fibers were hard to come by.

For awhile D'Arcy was sent with an experienced worker to collect the pitch, which was slowly oozing from gashes cut into the pine trees. After the collection was finished, every worker helped with the production of tar.

The pine tree roots had to be grubbed out of the soft black swamp soil and heated to roast out the tar. Then the tar was collected, put into barrels, or hogsheads, and stacked until a ship was loading to sail to England.

Oddly enough, this labor was far less discouraging than brick work or fishing. The roots came out fairly readily from the swamp muck. Stoking the fires and adding the roots to the tent-like roasting piles was slow, easy work. Meanwhile, he roamed about checking to see that the oozing pitch was falling squarely into the bark containers. It would be a challenge to fail in this work.

Was he to find his place in the collection of naval stores? In this oddly happy frame of mind, his day passed. His hands became stained black from the dried pitch and the swamp soil. He smelled of sweat and smoke and tar as daylight faded over the James.

Guardsman

Said the sergeant of the guard, "Ye take the watch this night. The safety o' the fort, and all that lie therein, rests in the likes o' ye watchmen. Guard it well."

With this daily plunge into one new activity after another, D'Arcy had given little thought to the manning of the fort itself. Consequently, it was a shock to be approached on this particular evening with news that he had the duty until morning.

As he got to his feet and left his hut following the sergeant, he felt panic steal over him. Stand watch! Since the time he had arrived, he had been aware that there were men on guard at the gate and at each of the three raised and rounded angles of the triangular fort. But never had he dreamed that this responsibility would befall him! The guardsmen were as much a part of Jamestown as the palisades around it, as much a part of the scene as the pines beyond.

What did one do to stand guard? As they neared the guard house, he prayed that the sergeant or Captain Pierce would give him some instruction. "Do not let me fail!" a voice within him cried so loudly that surely the sergeant could hear. "Tell me, what does a man on duty up there do?" he pleaded silently.

Why tonight? He thought of the hours he had already toiled in the Pitch and Tar Swamp. Jamie would be disappointed that they could not keep to their plan to write their letter. How did they choose the guards? Would he be able to keep awake after the hours and hours of checking sap cups, grubbing out roots, and stoking the roasting fires? What was the punishment for falling asleep on duty? Instinctively he knew it would be worse than the torturing stocks. Dawn seemed very far away as the sergeant led him into the guard house.

A steel doublet was found that fitted him more or less. It was not the one he had been required to bring, as that armor had been issued to a man now away on an exploring party. This one was larger and weighed some fifteen pounds. A steel helmet was located to protect his head.

To protect his head! Would that be from an Indian arrow? From a flint-tipped arrow that might come winging its way from a deep shadow on the edge of the woods?

"Duty only temporary. Shorthanded. Got several men taken sick. A blast from this musket will kill the intruder, summon me, turn out the soldiers," stated the sergeant. He now handed D'Arcy musket and shot, waved an arm toward the angle of the fort to be manned, and trudged off into the night.

Up the ramp inside the wall of the fort D'Arcy climbed. His was the angle overlooking the downriver sector. The moon was his only friend tonight, and by her light he watched over the shadowy shore and his view of the river. He had no idea who the other two men were at the other angles. There was to be no communication with them apparently.

Nothing moved. Hour after hour a certain pride in his duty kept him awake and alert. As his weariness increased, fear of another failure and more ridicule kept him awake. The wind rose long after midnight, and tossing branches often made him think that he saw unnatural movements. After the wind diminished, there came a stillness that nearly paralyzed him, for the whole fort area was as quiet as a painting. In his fatigue, he thought of himself as a part of a still life like that one by a Dutch painter that hung in his father's hall.

He wished his imagination were not so active. Since he had arrived, he had rarely heard anybody mention the possibility that the Spanish might attack. The Indians were a source of constant danger and overpowering in number. Most colonists avoided talking about them as a menace, but they lived with the threat of angry Indians. So dark. How could he be certain that nothing moved?

At this moment the eastern sky began to change, and he riveted his attention on the changing sky as dawn moved in from the Atlantic. A cock crowed. Before long the first rays of the sun would find the fort and the houses beyond already scenes of activity. D'Arcy's eyes were gritty with fatigue as the light grew brighter.

A new day was dawning that would bring more honor and glory to England and to King James. Would the king, on this March day in 1619, give one passing thought to his struggling outpost in Virginia? People were beginning to emerge from their dwellings to draw water from the wells, to feed the hens and livestock. There was the smell of the smoke of replenished fires. The clamor of the birds was reaching its peak.

Was this the time when Indians would choose to attack?

The chilling thought made D'Arcy forget the dreadful weight of his armor. He even forgot how his head and neck ached from the heavy helmet. The possibility of an enemy waiting out there in dew-dampened thickets, just within arrow range, kept him wide awake until his relief arrived.

A Letter for Jamie

On the basis of twenty-four hours of wakefulness in labor and guard duty, D'Arcy was excused from church. After a porringer of hot cornmeal mush with goat's milk and a gourd of cool water, he went to his hut and was soon asleep, oblivious to the activities going on that day.

The total of these days' accomplishments was making history. One day people would look down the years to Jamestown and call it the first successful and permanent English settlement in the New World.

During that day axes sounded in the woodlands. Some men were gathering reeds for thatching new buildings. Some tended tobacco fields or drove the crows from cornfields now being planted with the new crop. The few women were attending household chores. The crack of the hunters' muskets echoed and re-echoed across the James, as ducks were shot for the evening meal. There were men who carried bricks, some who fished, and some who added to the naval stores. Indians came to trade and walked about the settlement with no restrictions. The governor and his council pondered the problems of the colony, but D'Arcy slept through it all.

"Wake up, Mr. Southall. Come and have roast duck. We have been cookin' them ever so long. They smell very savory. It is near time for service, then we will sup, and we may write the letter tonight. Open your eyes, do!"

Who could still be asleep? The boy's eager chatter made him aware of hunger, that he must not be tardy for church, and that at last they could write the letter. He rose, yawned, dressed, splashed cold water on his face, and followed Jamie into the rapidly filling church.

Later they sat at the communal table. As the steaming food was served, D'Arcy listened with interest to the events of the day. Two deer had been taken along with the ducks, the fishing catch was above expectations with two sturgeons and many herring among the usual varieties, and a new brick wall was finished.

"The duck is well roasted, Jamie. I never had better."

"It is the wood we use—a kind that yields nuts also. Hickory it is called."

"H-m-m, hickory smoke for roasting meat. I suppose we shall become quite fond of it as time goes by."

"Dickin had good luck with the new batch of ale, they say. Would ye like me to fetch ye a draught?"

"A small one would be good tonight. So Dickin is our master brewer, is he?" The ale was better than he could have hoped, for Dickin was managing well with his make-do apparatus. "My compliments to the brewmaster," he said with a smile.

When Jamie returned from his little errand, D'Arcy said, "Come now, we have a while until sundown to pen your letter." They gathered paper, quill, ink, and a book to write upon from D'Arcy's sea chest and withdrew to a quiet place beside the river.

This was an experience that D'Arcy had not clearly foreseen. Jamie had been brave and cheerful enough when he believed that the ties with home and family were severed forever. But the idea of sending a message home was prompting waves of homesickness. Words tumbled from trembling lips. In the end he had a good cry while D'Arcy put down the final words in his careful hand. This proved to be as hard as anything he had as yet attempted.

"There! 'Tis done. Would you like to hear what you have said?" And he read it.

"Me very words! Preserved they are for anyone to read who kens the magic!"

"Magic again, Jamie? There is no magic here—just learning and using what you learn. See here. You learned today to cook ducks. Next time it will seem easier, and you will use some of those same skills to cook other meats. You then branch out to cook fish, bread, and soups, do you not? In writing and reading you also learn a bit at a time. You branch out as you learn. Do you understand?"

"No, not entirely, sir."

"It is learning a bit at a time every day."

"Will you teach me?"

The very breeze seemed to hold its breath until D'Arcy replied with his warmest, friendliest grin, "I will, Jamie."

Here was a task that he could begin with hope of success. "My need to teach is as great as yours to learn."

"What you say is too grown-up for me to ken. I cannot find your meaning. You say you are willing to show me how to read words. Or is it to write them? Which comes first?"

"To read is to write, and to write is to read 'Tis a picture of thought and the spoken word. Let us begin."

The days passed pleasantly. Processing the pitch and pine stumps or hovering over the smoky swamp fires seemed to be good work. There was no promise of a great future here, but it was satisfying to watch the hogsheads of tar and pitch being readied for a home-bound ship. Those extremely long pine trunks would be lashed to the ship's side and would become a part of great ships.

He tried to imagine these newest merchantmen of the East India Company. What adventures they would encounter on the run to the Cape of Good Hope and across the Indian Ocean to India! He could picture these areas on a map, but what were these places actually like? They are as different as this America is from what he had imagined it to be. He felt a ripple of excitement as another of the hogsheads he had helped to prepare was trundled off to the storage area, for he was making a contribution to the growing navy and trading fleet for a mightier England.

In the evenings other men, hearing of the letter he had written for Jamie, were seeking his help to write to their loved ones. And these messages, like the naval stores, amassing daily because of his efforts, awaited the next sailing. Although he had never considered himself a scholar, there were few in Jamestown who were better trained in the literary arts.

Yeardley, the New Governor

In April Jamestown was in a fair turmoil. Governor Argall was departing before the expected arrival of his successor, Sir George Yeardley. It was an odd situation.

Sir George had previously come to Virginia as captain of the military guard under Governor Thomas Gates. Yeardley and Argall had become friends in 1610 when Argall was the captain of Governor De La Warr's flagship. In fact, they had become such good friends that Yeardley had named his first born Argoll. Why was there to be no meeting now of the two men?

Rumors of mismanaged affairs by Governor Argall were spreading. It was said that Argall had left no records at all for his successor. D'Arcy decided to wait for more facts before criticizing the man. He regarded the governor's position a difficult one. He felt sorry for any man who had so many difficult people with whom to deal.

The fact that his superiors were a year away made the governor's work very difficult. A question from him took several weeks, perhaps months, to reach England. A presentation to the Virginia Company and a decision from that body took more time, and then the answer could be expected back in Virginia about a year from the time the question was asked.

Governor George Yeardley, his pretty wife, Lady Temperance, and little Argoll, nearly nine months old, arrived in late April 1619. It was the first time in ten years that a governor's wife had joined her husband in the colony. No governor's lady had yet lived in the brick and seasoned timber house that had been prepared for Governor Gates' family, as his wife had died during the voyage from England.

Immediately Governor Yeardley put the colony on the alert for a possible Indian attack. He was a soldier by profession, and he had first hand knowledge of the defenses. On earlier duty in the colony he had helped to build the forts at the entrance to Chesapeake Bay, Fort Henry, and Fort Charles. In April 1611 he was one of the group sent upriver near the falls to construct the new town of Henricus with proper defenses.

Another rumor was that Yeardley was actually going to call an assembly of the colonists to decide on some of the problems bedeviling the whole James River region.

But most important, D'Arcy was thinking, as he watched the governor proceed to his seat at the front of the church, this Yeardley was getting his hands on large tracts of land. Consequently, his interests would be the same as the Virginians.

Trading with the Indians

One morning D'Arcy was assigned to a task that took him away from the Pitch and Tar Swamp. A body of men were provided with armor and guns. They were to carry a trunk load of objects to barter with the Indians for some much-needed corn, as harvest time was many months away.

Why he had been chosen he never knew, but after church service, devoted mostly to asking God's help in successful trading, the people were promptly served their communal meal. It was a hearty venison stew. Then the traders boarded a sloop and headed upriver.

This would be the first time D'Arcy had an opportunity to meet the Indians. Until today he had seen them at a distance or occasionally walking inside the palisade when they had some reason to see the colonists. What would it be like to deal with them? Would they act friendly or show bitterness that more and more of their land was being settled by the English?

As the wooded shore slipped past, towering pines whispered with the winds. Honeysuckle vines and holly trees made the undergrowth in the thickets intensely green. "May I never have to make my way through that tangle!" commented D'Arcy to the man near him. "Look at the thorny underbrush!"

"Ha! See that black water swamp," replied the other.

"And God preserve us!" breathed D'Arcy. They watched a thick-bodied water snake swim across a stretch of that dark swamp water. As D'Arcy's eyes followed the fast, fluid motion of the reptile, a shiver rippled up his spine.

When the sloop had sailed far up the James, an Indian gathering came in sight. Several canoes came out to meet them and escort them to the shore. This was a temporary campsite for the exchange of trade goods.

Mostly they had baskets of beans in several varieties—nuts, dried fruits, and especially maize or corn. D'Arcy admired the baskets. He would like some of those for himself.

So these were the Algonquins. "The most amazing thing about them is their size. These men must be a good foot taller than ourselves," D'Arcy remarked.

"Big they may be, but that cannot compare with their amazingly sly and devious nature," his companion replied.

"They probably have a like opinion of us," said D'Arcy, "but look at that superb muscular development!"

"That is obvious enough since they are nearly naked. That bear's fat smeared on their bodies helps them to stand the insects and perhaps the cold weather, but it makes them smell loathsome to be near."

"If they have found a defense against these gnats," sighed D'Arcy, waving off a pesky swarm, "I may start wearing it this very day, smell or no smell!"

The two men joined the others where the trading was to take place. The men from Jamestown now opened their single trunk. D'Arcy felt ashamed of the pitiful things that they had brought to trade for the precious food. The Indians gave baskets of beans for a few yards of poorly dyed red cloth. Now for the most valuable commodity—the maize. Here was nourishing and satisfying food. Would the few trade items seem desirable enough, valuable enough, useful enough to trade for all the corn they needed?

From the trunk were laid out several mirrors, some blue and white beads, and now the knives: one, two, three. The Indians made signs that they wanted more: four, five. That was all there were.

How many days of working the land, seeding, hoeing, bird chasing, and harvesting had gone into the raising of this corn? How much labor, on the other hand, had gone into locating of iron ore, mining, smelting, and shaping those knives?

How precious seemed the razor-sharp knives to the men who had only sharpened stones for the skinning and cutting up of game! How precious the maize looked to the poorly stocked colonists!

D'Arcy slipped his own knife out and looked at it. He had had it for a very long time. He could replace it back at the fort. How many of those handy baskets could he get in return for this worn-out thing? So he began his own bargaining on the side. How was he to know that it would upset the delicate balance of trade?

At first the Indian did not understand that he wanted empty baskets. This caused no end of clamor and uneasiness and distrust. His companions resented his willingness to trade a perfectly good knife for such useless things as three empty baskets. These containers could as easily be purchased full of maize! The affair ended with everyone feeling cheated and out of sorts.

Sweaty under the heavy armor, tired, hungry, and provoked, the traders returned downriver, arriving just past sundown.

D'Arcy set the three baskets inside his hut to use henceforth as a place to store his belongings. They were large, strong, and cleverly woven. He was well pleased with his trade, but he would never again be sent on a trading venture among their Indian neighbors.

Yeardley and Rolfe

Sir George Yeardley, governor, appointed by the Virginia Company of London, was awaiting the arrival of his friend and councilman, John Rolfe. In the yard of his residence he strolled about, smoking his white clay pipe. He was looking at his new plantings of grapevines.

"Ah, there you are, John. I see that you have brought out your pipe too."

"That and a blend of tobacco that I wish you to try, Sir George."

"Of course, I shall try it, but this sweet-scented leaf of yours is ever my favorite. A blend you say. Now that is something new."

"Not at all, my friend. The Indians add bits of sumac and the inner bark of the dogwood tree to their strong tobacco. They call this *kinnikinnik*, their Algonquin word for *that which is mixed*."

"Little did we realize, John Rolfe, when we first set sail for this land in 1609 in the *Sea Venture* that so much would befall us! You learned about blending tobacco from your Pocahontas?"

"Yes," sighed Rolfe, "I mastered the art of mixing it from my little Indian wife, Chief Powhatan's favorite child. So you also have been thinking of our first voyage? Much has happened since we survived that shipwreck."

"Good stories we shall have for our grandchildren, eh? But let us get to the business at hand. I have acted on what I deem the most urgent needs of the colony since I arrived at planting time. After last year's drought, we must make every effort to produce a bountiful crop. It is a pleasure these June days to watch the corn and tobacco growing tall."

"Your sending the guardsmen into the fields to protect the planters was indeed the act of an old army man, Sir George. I know you must wish often that you were again the captain of the militia rather than the governor himself."

"I must gainsay it! No, John, I am well content to leave the militia to your father-in-law, Captain William Pierce. He is a good man for the job.

This brings us back to my orders that I dare not delay further in fulfilling. I must, now that it is already June, send out word that two members are to be elected from each hundred and plantation. They, together with the officials of the four boroughs, are to assemble here at Jamestown. When, think you, should we have them meet?

"I too have been thinking of this gathering of our freemen," said Rolfe. "It will take time for them to prepare for the meeting. The end of July would be as soon as it can now be arranged."

"I must meet with you councilmen to draw up a slate of problems that we must discuss. How long do you estimate the assembly will need to meet?"

"Some three days or more, I'd venture. Oh, I can hear now the moaning about meeting and the groaning about conducting business at the hottest time of the year."

"Alas, it will come at a frightfully uncomfortable time, and I considered that. But postpone it until cooler weather I dare not, John. For one thing we must increase our defenses against the Indians. The threat of an uprising is ever hanging over us, but the colonists tend to ignore it. If ever those huge fellows got themselves organized and had a leader to rile them up over their lost lands, we would be in terrible trouble. And I have reason to fear that they have found such a leader."

"It does not bear thinking of, Sir George. I pray that you are over-zealous, yet I can understand your deep concern. The safety of the colony is your prime responsibility. The people seem apathetic only because they do not want to live with fear."

"That is all the more reason to get on with this assembly."

"Ah, yes. You will expect the men...what should they be called? Members, representatives."

"A more distinctive name, I would myself prefer. Since they will be coming from their townships, or burgs, what think you of the term burger?"

"H-m-m. The burger of Smythe's hundred, or burgian...or burgess."

"Burgess! And the lot of them burgesses! That is it, John!"

"And the House of Burgesses gives the body a name equal in dignity to the House of Parliament in London. What do you think of this?" asked Rolfe with a delighted grin.

"Oh, that is excellent! Ah, for the first time on American soil a representation of the people will have a voice in their own affairs. Have you considered what this means?"

"I have, Sir George, for they will be more intent to live by laws they have a voice in making. It is our duty to make it a very fine occasion. What are your requirements as to dress and the manner of conducting the meetings?" The slender and elegant John Rolfe could be relied upon to think of these things. He and Pocahontas had been received in high society when he took his little family to London, where they were a credit to the colony.

"We should follow the House of Parliament. Yes, even to the clothing, although it will be very warm for July. The plumed hats."

"Hats to be worn in the meetings? Surely, Sir George."

"Hats will be worn, to be removed only when a burgess indicates a wish to speak. This is the way it was done, at a meeting of the Virginia Company that I attended. There were over six hundred members present, and it was very impressive."

"It will be most uncomfortable. It will be difficult to see what is going on, for it must be in the church where the meetings will be held." The two men smoked in silence for a time as they considered these plans. Rolfe continued, "Oh, when the notice is prepared for Kecoughtan, pray allow me to include an invitation for the two burgesses to be my houseguests. I feel certain that my friend, Captain William Tucker, will be one of those elected. I should greatly enjoy his company while he is here."

"Very well. This conversation has made me quite eager to get on with it! In the morning we shall prepare the notification for the first meeting of our House of Burgesses. It will not take long, as I gave it considerable thought when I was on the ship this spring."

"The messages should be dispatched by the last day of June," added Rolfe as he offered the governor more tobacco.

"This blend of yours is good—very good indeed."

As they refilled their pipes, they watched the fireflies twinkle in the thickets, and night came down the sky.

Silkworms

"Mr. Southall, have ye seen the silkworms today? The wee creatures are growin' that fast. I can almost watch them change. And do they never stop their munchin' o' the mulberry leaves at all, at all?"

Jamie joined D'Arcy for a sunset stroll along the edge of the James above the fort. The sky of gold and pink was reflected in this great, broad river. The water splashed the bank in soft, running waves. Their world was a beautiful place this July twilight.

"Ah, yes, the silkworms. These were sent us by the Virginia Company, you recall, to produce silk for an experiment. It is another way we may make a profit for our sponsors. But we are ever shorthanded, needing every person's labor to make Virginia a successful venture. We cannot spare people to give constant attention to the tending and feeding of those smelly little worms."

"So ye think we will be sendin' back very little silk? Here, have a piece of cornbread. There was some left after the evening meal."

"But not for long," laughed D'Arcy, accepting a piece. "You have some also, I see. Cook will send you off to nurse the silkworms if he catches you taking food!"

"Snitchin' is what makes it taste so good," mumbled Jamie with his mouth full. Then he grinned, D'Arcy thought, like a wicked little imp.

"Let us not break the rules again," munched D'Arcy. "Rules are made for the good of all. Like laws."

Jamie sighed. "Everybody is talking o' laws and the House o' Burgesses that is to meet on the morrow. Tell me what it is about. What will it mean to us?"

D'Arcy motioned toward a fallen tree that would make a good seat. Away to their right were the burnt out remains of the old glass factory that had been a disappointment long before they had arrived. "Let us watch the sunset from here. You should know that there are four boroughs in Virginia. Tell me what you can about them."

"The Borough of Kecoughtan is downriver at the mouth o' the James on the north bank," Jamie began. "That is the smallest one. We are the biggest, the Borough of James City with Jamestown in the middle of it."

"And remember," added D'Arcy, "it stretches far on both sides of the river. Go on."

"I have heard about the great plantations up and down river. Then comes the Borough of Charles City upriver on both banks. It was named for Prince Charles. The Borough o' Henricus is beyond, up near the falls o' the river. That was named for our King James' older son Henry, who would have been our next king. But he died."

"You did well. Now when Governor Yeardley came, he had orders from the Virginia Company to organize a civilian government and to begin by calling together a general assembly. We call it the House of Burgesses also. Each plantation and each hundred have elected two men. The boroughs have officials representing them. All twenty-two men are here in Jamestown tonight."

"What will they do when they meet in the church tomorrow?"

"They are to read over our great charter and to advise the Virginia Company and the King of changes that are now deemed necessary."

"This great charter is what you are writing now, is it not?" asked Jamie, looking with great pride at his friend.

"Do not overrate me, lad," D'Arcy laughed. "It is true that I am working as the clerk of Secretary John Pory these days. The governor has set us the task of making four copies of the great charter so that committees will be able to work on different parts of it. He will have many papers to prepare over the next few days, and I have been asked to assist him."

"That is because not many can write as well as we can."

D'Arcy laughed and tousled the hair of his eager pupil and continued. "The House of Burgesses is to set up a government that will pass laws and hold court. Of course, we shall be under the same laws as those of England. Soon the laws will make clear who owns the tracts of land, and it will, at last, be possible for those eligible to purchase land. Then too, the Burgesses will look through all the orders given to our earlier governors to see what practices should continue, and which ones are no longer necessary."

"How will the men vote?"

"A carpenter has made a fine box with a secret chamber. To vote *aye*, a man drops in a white ball. To vote *nay*, he puts in a black one. Then the secret part is opened and the twenty-two balls will tell how the matter is decided."

Jamie's eyes were shining as he listened to how the box with the secret chamber was to be used. "What will happen after they vote on all the business?"

"The colony will live under and obey the laws and accept the decisions. All the records on the meeting will be written down for us to keep here in

Jamestown. Copies will be sent to London for the Virginia Company and for the king to read and approve…or advise us to change."

"How many of us are there in Virginia now?"

"We number over four thousand, Jamie."

"You are going to the meeting, are you not?"

"Yes, I have been asked to help record what the burgesses say. Secretary Pory needs assistance, and it is a great honor for me to have even a small part in this first meeting of the House of Burgesses. Come, lad, it is time we return to the fort."

"You were kind to explain all o' this to me," said Jamie as they ambled toward the palisades. "Do you think silkworms go to sleep?"

The First House of Burgesses

Drum beats pulsed through the heavy, moist air. D'Arcy had shrugged to make his best coat fit more smoothly over his shirt, which was damp from the early morning air when he put it on while it was still dark. He had put on his hat and joined Secretary Pory and the burgesses for a very early breakfast. It would be a long, hot day. He sighed and headed for the church as the drum beat throbbed. It was an hour after sunrise on July 30, 1619.

If D'Arcy noticed the darkly handsome burgess of Kecoughtan, William Tucker, guest of Councilman John Rolfe, it was only as a member of the company. The time would come when he would wish that he had been more observant.

The church had been divested of its religious objects and rearranged for the meeting. Reverend Buck waited patiently as the men took their places. Then he led them in prayer, beseeching God to bless the work of these men meeting together. He asked that they be humble of heart as they set up this new form of government, wherein the people themselves would have a voice in deciding necessary laws. His voice shook with emotion as he begged the burgesses to work with respect for each other to find agreement on difficult problems that they must discuss. "In God's name, amen," he finished and departed.

"Below that window," whispered Jamie later in the morning, "is where we should be able to hear."

Giles, an orphan who had recently been sent to the colony and was another of Cook's helpers, nodded. "Cook will be ragin' mad that we run off. Ow-w-w I kin 'ear me 'ead buzzin' like a 'ive o' bees when 'e knocks our 'eads together, Jamie."

"This time it will be worth it! I do not want to miss this. Come on if you're comin'."

Together they crept to the church wall and crouched very quietly in the shadow by the open casement. Jamie knew Cook would have missed them by now. He would be in a fair tizzy with all the burgesses coming to table at midday and expecting the best of food in the recess of their labors. The governor had made this very clear indeed, and Jamie knew it.

The boys listened as the voices within the church talked of several committees, which were to read the great charter. The committees were directed to bring back recommendations to the entire body to retain or delete the original plans. It was just as D'Arcy had described. Giles was getting restless. Better to give him something to do. "Lift me up so I can see all the burgesses together, Giles. Do!"

D'Arcy was amused to see Jamie's head appear suddenly and briefly above the wind hole, but nobody else apparently had noticed. "The rascal! Our talk last night must have impressed him," he thought. "Now if those boys will only be quiet, they can hear some of this historic discussion." He was writing steadily about land grants and the need for surveying.

Thinking of the punishment that he was sure was coming, Giles decided to enjoy some fun first. He jabbed his elbow into Jamie's side and received one back. He added a little punch and a shove next, and Jamie jumped on him, sending him against the church wall with a thud. Without thinking, they were suddenly wrestling in the crunchy, old weathered leaves.

Inside the sounds of scuffling reached the ears of the burgesses. Some remembered having been boys themselves and grinned, glad enough of the interruption to the weighty matters. Some frowned at the disturbance. The governor spoke to the guardsman behind his chair, "Do you step outside and clear the area of any boys near our wind holes. The meeting will continue, Gentlemen."

Jamie had gotten a fine hold on Giles and had him properly pinned down, when a pair of guardsman's legs appeared beside him.

"Up, you fellows! Be off in the governor's name!" Then the guardsman winked at them as they sheepishly rose. They grinned and raced off to their irate master and to the unbearable cooking fires, while the guardsman sighed and returned to his wearisome duty, standing in heavy armor holding his upraised halberd, behind the governor.

From the hour after sunrise to the hour before sunset, the burgesses met July 30, 31, August l, 2, 3, and ended their work on August 4.

Jamie missed hearing that a tax of a pound of tobacco (for each man over sixteen) had been approved to pay the expenses of this meeting and that each homeowner was to keep extra corn on hand to exchange for other goods, if this food were needed for new arrivals in the colony.

A message was worded to send to London respectfully asking the Virginia Company to approve their decisions and thanking the company for the privilege of holding this meeting.

They were discussing how they were to educate the Indians and convert them to Christianity. Just then a pair of tiny kids came bleating and leaping past the church, paused, and proceeded through the trees toward the riverbank. The governor lifted an eyebrow at John Rolfe, who was trying to maintain his dignity. It had been John who had suggested that a guardsman be posted at the church door to prevent any such disgraceful disturbance such as domestic animals gamboling through the meeting. Now Yeardley was thanking his lucky stars for such a practical man as John, his councilman, his friend.

D'Arcy thought of Jamie as he recorded the suggestion of the burgess of Kecoughtan that the borough be renamed Elizabeth City in honor of the princess. If approved, all of King James' children would then have boroughs named for them.

At last the business turned from lawmaking to law enforcement. A murder trial involved a ship's mate, killed at Smythe's Hundred. The twelve-man jury found the man in charge at Smythe's guilty, but he received a suspended sentence.

Then Henry Spellman was tried for treason. He was an Indian interpreter, who had spoken of Governor Yeardley in a belittling manner to the Indians. His punishment was to work without pay for seven years.

D'Arcy marveled at the way the men kept their minds on the work in spite of the wasps that hovered in the warm air. They flew about the heads of everybody sooner or later. One landed on his hand, and he kept very still while it walked about, leaving an itchy little path. The flies were such pests! Many a time he had to wave a hand to dislodge them from his papers, or had been distracted as they buzzed past.

With plans to meet the next March, the weary men now listened to their governor commend their fine work and willingness to cooperate with one another. He urged them to be ever watchful of the neighboring Indians. Then the first meeting of the House of Burgesses was over.

Governor Yeardley and Councilman Rolfe exchanged smiles as the burgesses followed them from the church. They were proud of the success of this assembly. The colony had now passed from a government under martial law to a civilian government. The people's representatives would make their own laws, subject to the approval of the Virginia Company and the king. At last the colonists could own land. The change in the Virginia Company's chief officer of treasurer from Sir Thomas Smith to Sir Edwin Sandys had resulted in a refreshing change in policy for the Virginians.

D'Arcy put down his quill pen. He rose to move his stiff shoulders. He clenched his hand to relieve the cramps caused by steady writing. He heard the burgesses, wonderfully revived now that the meeting had ended, talk of going home.

"We are to have the evening meal and one last night here together," D'Arcy overheard a burgess say. "Then we leave early on the morn for our homes. The governor insists that we travel by daylight, and says he would not like to hear of any of us being overtaken by the Indians after dark. Do you suppose that he thinks the Indians have been keeping an eye on our meeting here?"

The governor was as eager to depart as the burgesses. On the next day he would be off to see the tobacco fields that were growing his salary at Argall Town. He would visit Smythe Hundred, where he was responsible for the corporate farm, as each man would receive a share of half of the tobacco grown. The rest of the crop would repay some of the members of the Virginia Company for their investments. He was the paid manager and held stock in this hundred. His chief interest was his share in Flowerdieu Hundred, which lay on the south side of the James, across from Argall Town. How he looked forward to a few days' rest as he visited his lands up the broad, sunny river, where cooling breezes ruffled the surface!

D'Arcy's duties were far from over.

"You will meet with me early in the morn. We must prepare papers on this meeting for the Virginia Company. The governor will expect them well advanced on his return from upriver, and they are to be ready for the next sailing. Sir Edwin Sandys will be waiting," said Mr. Pory.

Thanksgiving

On the last day of November in 1619 the *Margaret* was sighted coming up the James. She had been at sea since September 16th and had made the crossing with uncommon good fortune under the command of Captain John Woodliffe. The men of Jamestown gave him a rousing welcome. Many a knowing head nodded respect to the man who could log a two-and-a-half-month voyage from England, despite the hurricane season.

For a few days the ship anchored there as the restless seafarers swarmed ashore and stretched their legs on tours of the settlement. Some of the men thoroughly enjoyed duck hunting. But Captain Woodliffe was eager to off-load the messages and supplies he carried in order to proceed to his destination, Berkeley Plantation.

Woodliffe was commander of this new plantation of 8,000 acres with a river frontage of three miles. His ship carried settlers and supplies to start a settlement on this tobacco land, recently acquired upriver by a group that included Richard Berkeley.

On December 3rd the ship departed. Reverend Buck chose as his topic that morning the text of the charter for the Berkeley lands, which ordered the day of the settlers' arrival to be a day of thanksgiving. That date "shall be yearly and perpetually kept holy as a day of thanksgiving to Almighty God." He offered a moving prayer that this would become an annual occasion for divine services and joyous feasting throughout all present and future English colonies.

D'Arcy walked across the island to resume his work in the Pitch and Tar Swamp. As he helped to stack the pine roots for roasting out the tar, he wished he had been on that departing ship. To be present at the start of a plantation, as well as to be part of that thanksgiving, would have been a fine change from the routine life around here. He let his imagination follow the ship.

The band of thirty-eight men was disembarking. The frigid wavelets, driven by the brisk fall wind, threatened to soak their feet. Overhead in the towering pines there was a roaring of the wind that rose and fell plaintively. If Jamestown had looked like the end of the civilized world to these men a few days ago, now it seemed to represent a home place, wherein there were warm dwellings, good fellowship, and the whole well managed and secure.

Woodliffe saw the stricken expressions, the lonely look in the eyes, and perhaps he also had a moment of homesickness. Straightway he commanded the company to kneel there on the pine strewn shore to hold their devotional service.

With the day already well spent, the men needed little encouragement to set about providing for their needs. They would sleep aboard the ship, but wood and water must be gathered quickly, for who would wish to go beyond the light of the fires, once early dusk began to fall?

The fires were the center of community life. Their warmth and light cheered the dark afternoon. In heartwarming companionship the men gathered about them. The thanksgiving feast was broiled and roasted in their glowing coals. The savory meats, salted with the product of the colony's own salt-drying works on the Eastern Shore, were eaten within the light and warmth of the fires.

As the settlers rowed back to the *Margaret*, the early night was darkening. Across the water from the wilds they heard for the first time the keening howl of wolves.

D'Arcy looked around his familiar Pitch and Tar Swamp. Ah, that would be a lonely place to live! Berkeley was too close to the wolves and bears. The Indians were much too near such an isolated and undefended location.

Jamestown was the best place to live. Here was the very center of activities, and one knew what was going on.

D'Arcy felt good as he warmed his hands by the fire and then kicked a smoldering root nearer the flame.

Maids Acomin'

Jamie was running with all his might toward the smoke columns in the Pitch and Tar Swamp. He was remembering what D'Arcy had told him about lifting his knees to lengthen his stride. "Mr. Southall! Mr. Southall! There's a rumor...that the governor...has received word...that a hundred maids...are acomin' to be wives!"

"Well now, that should liven up this river bank."

Jamie's flushed, excited face fell. "Is that all you can say? Up at the fort they are fair reelin' with the news. What is wrong?"

"Can you imagine me taking a wife now? I scarcely do enough to rate my own food and lodging. These women are for men more established than I am, Jamie. All I can claim in land is fifty acres because I paid my own passage across the sea. That is called a headright, you know. Until I have earned the right to more acreage, I do not wish to make a claim."

"You served as a clerk at the assembly. Surely you can possess enough to equal 125 pounds of tobacco by the time they come."

"Oh? The bridegroom is to pay that amount for the bride's passage? It is not the first expense that would deter me. I have no home in which to set her up, and I have no very profitable labor. Do you understand?"

Why did D'Arcy heave that pine root, as if it had angered him, onto the pile awaiting the roasting fire? This was so unlike him, Jamie thought.

And since the early spring of 1620 still had many a cold day, D'Arcy would make no move to seek other employment. The fires gave a comfort much envied by other work parties. It was one way to help ward off the chills and fevers that plagued the colony. Those screaming winds that lashed the James into whitecaps and roused a roaring in the tall pines passed over the Pitch and Tar Swamp. Down here the reeds and rushes held something of the warmth from the sun and the fires.

Whenever he could be spared from the preparation of meals, Jamie would take a welcome run out the gate, around to the north side of the fort, and down to the swamp. He would stop at the creek long enough to look for the sharp little paw prints of raccoons in the muddy bank. Now he was enjoying watching D'Arcy ladle tar into a hogshead.

"That is a fine, rich sauce you are makin'."

"As you see, I am making progress with my cooking just as you are with yours."

"But you are the lucky one. You make your tar the same each time, never havin' to think about things moldin' or sourin' or curdlin' or rottin' or gettin' nibbled by bugs and mice."

"Why, I never thought about that, lad. You cooks have more ways of spoiling our meals than I have given you proper credit for!"

"Ha! Listen to the man! What do y' think everyone from the governor on down to Giles would be sayin' if we cooks wasted any o' the food that the work parties bring in? Or if we spoiled in the cookin' any of last fall's great harvest? That was the best in the past twelve years, they say."

"You would hardly be the most popular fellows in Jamestown. You might even be set to amuse yourselves in the stocks...until we got hungry again, of course. What are you getting ready for—our midday meal? This work in the pines makes a man royally hungry."

"Oysters today. I must be off to help with the roastin'. Is there any way that pitch and tar can spoil?"

"It will not separate nor sour, if that is what you mean. But it will burn with a most furious and intense heat. I never want to be on a ship at sea should fire reach the holds where these hogsheads are stored."

"Oh-h-h, think o' that now! It makes me think how well off we are manning the king's fort," and away he sped.

Why was it that Jamie could be satisfied and happy, feeling the importance of the work he was doing? D'Arcy picked up his wooden mallet and hammered the top on the hogshead with his mouth set in a grim line.

"Here I am," he reflected, "doing my share in this work party. I am teaching Jamie to read and write besides writing letters home for others. Some things bear remembering like helping old Pory as clerk and that night I stood double guard duty. What a newcomer I was in those days! My life has few of the comforts I knew in my father's house, but I am glad I came. This is a pleasant land and an exciting one. One never knows what will take place from day to day. But I want to do more than man the king's fort. Now how do I go about it?"

And All the Men and Women...

April came at last. One morning a little sloop sailed merrily up to the moorings near the fort. She brought word that the ships bearing the maidens had been sighted down the Chesapeake. What a flurry this news caused!

A holiday mood swept through the settlement. Lady Temperance Yeardley put everybody within hailing distance to work on the reception she was preparing. Food for a great feast was rushed to the cooks. Such a searching for presentable clothing went on! Such a hurry to clean up, to trim hair and beards, to make the fort look festive! The few women were trying to make it clear that some badly needed housecleaning would impress the maids far more than dressy bunting. The sun came out to accent the marvelous beauty of magenta redbud and white dogwood trees in the woodlands. Nearer and nearer were coming the ships bringing a hundred young women seeking husbands.

Here in Jamestown and along the river were hundreds of young men who were eager to see English women again and to establish family life in a land that promised prosperity to those hale and ambitious. Opportunities were here, but women were needed for family life at last.

As the two ships hove in sight, a cheer rose, which the maidens could not possibly have heard at such a distance. The *Jonathan* and the *London Merchant* grew in size as they came up the beautiful blue waters of the James.

D'Arcy stood back and watched as one might view a play, for all this had nothing to do with him. He found himself enjoying the little dramas going on around him much as he had been amused those long-ago evenings at the Globe Theatre in London. With friends he had gone to some of Shakespeare's plays, and lines from one of them came to him now:

All the world's a stage
And all the men and women merely players...
As You Like It 2.7.9.1-2

Governor and Lady Yeardley were at hand to welcome the maidens. He would soon read publicly the rules and regulations on arranging marriages. The young women were to live in huts prepared for them or with friends at Jamestown, while some would be sent on to other settlements: Charles City, Kecoughtan, and Henricus. The ships drew nearer the moorings. D'Arcy moved nearer the landing area in spite of himself.

He watched the other men acting like schoolboys on holiday. Then he looked at the maids lining the ships' rails. They too were all aflutter. Ribbons and laces, shawls and veils in all colors were tossing on the river breeze. Lilting voices, squeals, laughter, lively chatter, and a hundred pairs of little hands were trying to control the fluttering finery, betraying their excitement.

As the maidens began to come ashore, D'Arcy watched with an amused smile. On and on they moved, propelled by those ashore toward the reception. They were already mingling with the throng ashore. Some were being greeted by their fiancés, for several marriages had already been arranged in England before the men had left. Screams of recognition and hails of welcome from men who had planned to meet these maidens added to the din. Some of the maids, however, were trying hard not to look curious, but they were eager to look over at last the men who would soon be their husbands. That was the last of the young ladies aboard the *Jonathan*.

The *London Merchant* was discharging its passengers now. The thinning crowd regrouped to welcome this second and last shipload of young women. D'Arcy was closer this time to the gangplank, pushed forward by the crowd. Maid after maid reached firm land from the tipsy gangplank. Always a hand reached out to help her ashore. This was apparently the last. There was no reason to stay longer.

"And so," he mused, "all have left Pandora's box! There was not one in the lot I'd choose. More troubles than blessings there, I'd say."

"Could you help me, please?"

One had been left behind! She looked as if she had just awakened, for her eyes were still dazed and starry from sleep—with eyes as blue as the spring sky. Fair, curly hair caught and held the sun, as wisps blew across a rosy cheek. "I'm having trouble with the lid of my box."

"Naturally," D'Arcy replied, feeling rather bemused, as he leaped up the gangplank to adjust the latch on the little box she was carrying ashore.

"The others all went away and left me when I was asleep."

"I had supposed that it was something like that," he said, wondering if the fact that she was so attractive was the reason why she had been allowed to sleep on.

"What is your name?" he asked with an eagerness that startled them both.

"Becky. Rebecca Cox."

"Oh," he sighed with relief, "I was hoping against Hope."

"I beg your pardon?"

"Pandora would have understood."

"Pandora? Which ship? I thought I knew all their names."

"She was not on either ship."

"Oh…one of your lady friends then?"

"Why yes!" He was enjoying this immensely. "She lived hundreds and hundreds of years ago. If she lived at all."

"Oh! This is all Greek to me!"

"Precisely. There is a Greek myth about her. I shall tell you all about it one day if you like. But would you not like to go ashore now? The governor's lady is waiting."

She wavered slightly as her foot touched the unyielding land. D'Arcy's arms were around her. "Welcome to Jamestown, Becky." He kissed her lightly. "No longer strangers, but not yet friends. I am D'Arcy Southall."

"Were…had you been waiting for one of the passengers?"

"No, not I. But this was the main event today—to welcome all of you. Some men have been awaiting the maids quite eagerly, I must say."

"And some maids received a very warm welcome indeed, Mr. Southall."

"D'Arcy?"

"D'Arcy," she smiled up at him. She liked his eyes and his smile. Amusing and handsome both. Were they all like this?

To him the fort had never looked anything but somber and practical. Today it seemed like a stage setting.

> And all the men and women merely players,
> They have their exits and their entrances…
> *As You Like It 2.7.9.2-3*

Shakespeare again providing the fitting line. He looked down at the adorable girl on his arm, and another line from a play came hauntingly back to him, like cloud cover that follows sunlight:

> Life's but a walking shadow, a poor player
> That struts and frets his hour upon the stage
> And then is heard no more…
> *Macbeth* 5.5.5.8-10

A chill swept through him. He had had no intention of making the acquaintance of any of these young women. Yet here he was, behaving like the most ardent of the marriageable men! He had nothing to offer her! Turn her free! Let her meet a man who really wants and needs a wife—one who has his house built and his fields sown!

Her arm was light on his as they strolled about after the reception. She felt so natural beside him. He thought of his experiences in Jamestown: his illness, the unaccustomed menial labor, the failures, the lack of all that is comfortable or attractive in human living. All these, he now realized, had taxed him almost to the limits of his endurance.

But now. Now was the time to tell her that he had no right to encourage her friendship. And yet...he could not bring himself to turn her loose into this courtship arena! He could think of no man here worthy of her.

D'Arcy knew then that he wanted Becky beside him, as he had wanted nothing else since the day he landed at Jamestown.

While he showed her about the fort, he studied her features, her expressions, the way her hair tossed when a breeze caught loose tendrils. He wanted to remember how she looked and moved and spoke. "Where will you stay?"

"With the Rolfes. John recently married my cousin, Jane, and they have invited me to be their guest."

"Ah, there are the bells for church. Will you be able to stand for the whole time?" His voice was full of concern, as he recalled what an ordeal this had been on his first day. To be sure, he had been suffering the onset of that near-fatal fever. The women must stand at the rear of the church, and it would grow hot back there in such a throng. "I shall sit in the back row so that you can lean on me, if you should need to do so." He gave her a caring smile.

"D'Arcy, are you always this farseeing?"

"Today I cannot see beyond you, and I think you know it."

The service seemed long. Toward the end a hand did indeed rest on his shoulder. Its irregular pressure told him that she was getting increasingly unsteady on her feet. He was glad he could give her this little help. Pray God, it was enough to keep her from making a spectacle of herself! And then he prayed from a troubled heart, "Help me, Heavenly Father, to do what is best for her. Help me to win her love, without making a public display of our feelings such as these others are doing."

It was over. In the interval before the feast, he strolled with her down the river shore where new homes had not as yet been built. The pines sighed sweetly overhead. Mockingbirds, flashing their white markings, fascinated Becky. One sang nearby.

"How delightful it is down here!" sighed Becky. "It is pleasant to be away from people after all those weeks at sea. This welcome that Jamestown is giving us is wonderfully enthusiastic, but how good it is to be apart from the milling people and the noise!"

"It is my pleasure to introduce you to the peaceful beauty of your new homeland. I have another reason for bringing you here. Time is short, as the feast is about to begin. This scene I prefer to play without an audience, Becky. Is there any chance that you may learn to love me?" His world stood still, and even the bird held its song.

With a whirl of skirts, she was in his arms.

"And to think that this morning I did not know that she existed," he thought as his arms tightened about her.

The Rolfes

John Rolfe seated himself across the hearth from D'Arcy and filled his long white clay pipe. His wife, Jane, leaned forward to light a sliver of wood in the fire and applied the tiny flame to the tobacco fragments in his pipe. The sweet blue cloud rose, drifting past D'Arcy and Becky as he asked, "So far you have found no satisfying and profitable employment in the colony?"

"I have nothing that would enable me to provide a home for Becky as yet. An idea has occurred to us. Becky, tell how it came about."

"We were walking through the fort. From time to time men would call to D'Arcy, teasing him for having me on his arm. Then they would ask him to write letters for them. It seems they cannot write the news that they have found brides. Many of the maids' families are awaiting news as well. D'Arcy will be busy with all these letters to prepare for the next sailing."

"Yes, I can see the need for a public scribe," replied Rolfe. "There should be good pay in it as a part-time job. You were also employed as a clerk when the House of Burgesses met, as I recall."

"When this flurry of letters is over, I wish to do something about this awful need, sir. Surely we are not going to allow the children to grow up here so unlettered, are we?"

"This is one of our many concerns, and one that cannot be long ignored. We have discussed plans for eventually establishing a college, but it is how to reach the little children that is a great problem. The plantations are spreading out, both up and down the James, and too far apart to gather the little ones daily in school."

"So each plantation must have its own tutor! This is what I should like to be! Do you know of a planter who would engage me to teach his children? Becky would help his wife. In this way we would be sure of a home and livelihood. I could marry Becky without indenturing myself to a planter or to a craftsman. I could not face seven years of that kind of slavery, sir, and could not possibly impose such a life on Becky. My work in collecting naval stores has too limited a future although I have found it gratifying to make a contribution to our growing sea power."

"You will be missed in the swamp," said John. "I shall make inquiries as to the need for a tutor. It is fortunate that so many of the planters are still at Jamestown to welcome the maidens."

"Meanwhile, then, I shall write letters and pick up a few shillings thereby."

Now Becky withdrew to speak quietly with her cousin Jane.

"How are your indentured lads working out, Councilman? I had heard that you took some of the black men who came on a Dutch ship last August, just after the House of Burgesses met."

"They are learning fast on my land near Henrico. They should have a good future in tobacco. They will be freemen and can become landowners when they end their years of indenture."

"Freemen, you say, and landholders. Do we expect to take them into our society as full citizens with voting powers? In that instance, would it not necessitate educating them as to our language and customs?"

"You have raised questions that will be of great importance, particularly as this cheap labor is temptingly brought to our wharves by the Portuguese slavers. These ships have come in from time to time seeking markets for their human cargo. I do not pretend to know the answers to these questions."

"Would you say that slavery is a possibility in the future?"

"Either there will be slavery or a growing number of freed negroes, who will be seeking equal standing with the white populace. Their value as field hands will make their importation desirable in great numbers, I assure you, either as slaves or as indentured servants."

"Why have we not had this particular set of questions regarding the more numerous Indians?"

"You ask why we, unlike the Spaniards, have not enslaved the red men to do our menial labor, especially in raising tobacco? The Indian men simply will not work in the fields."

"But they are excellent farmers. We have been saved from starvation by their maize, squashes, and beans in all their white, red, black, and spotted varieties."

"Their men only prepare the fields, removing the trees, burning them over. It is the women who are the farmers, my friend, planting several crops in a single hill, in which they loosen the soil with a dibble stick. No, the care of the growing plants is women's work. Children and old men drive off the birds. Harvesting is again the work of women and children. All this is beneath the dignity of the Indian brave."

"What is to be the Indians' fate in competition with us, think you?"

"I believe that our gunpowder will triumph over their arrows eventually, and they will be driven westward, but not in our lifetime. Their numbers have already begun to lessen, as they fall sick with the diseases which we have brought, especially measles."

They watched a shower of sparks resolve into smoke and rise up the chimney. D'Arcy was aware that this was a conversation to remember. To have the opportunity to engage this knowledgeable man in responding to many of the questions that had come to mind was a rare privilege.

Rolfe was thinking that here was a young man who was learning about the colony by working shoulder to shoulder with the humblest and becoming well acquainted with people of many types. He had already come to appreciate the problems that had the councilmen pounding their fists on the conference table. If he had a desire to instruct children, well, why not indeed? They would learn more than the basic skills from his teaching.

"D'Arcy," inquired Jane, who had been silent until now, "are you not interested in claiming your headright? You are entitled now to 50 acres for each of you."

"This is what I plan to do when I feel more settled in my mind, know where I want to settle, and can lay claim to a larger tract through my services. I am well aware that last year we sent home 45,000 pounds of tobacco at three shillings a pound. And you, Sir, have taught me that 1,000 plants will yield about 112 pounds of marketable leaf. But before I start raising tobacco, I wish to start planting the *A B* Cs in the heads of our next generation."

"Have you done any teaching?" Jane asked.

"I have a pupil even now," D'Arcy answered with a happy grin. "Jamie is a lad of twelve and indentured to the chief cook. He is a clever boy and making rapid progress in reading and writing. Soon I shall start him in mathematics. I plan to ask my sister in London to send me the books that I left with her and more supplies for teaching."

"How far did you go in your education?" This was a question that Rolfe had been wishing to ask for some time.

"I had a year at Oxford, sir."

"We shall do all that we can to further your ambition, shall we not, John?" It was a comment that warmed D'Arcy's heart. He knew now that Jane approved of him for Becky.

"Now I must depart," said D'Arcy, rising and taking Becky's hand. "It will be a long time before I shall be able to provide my wife with a home as fine as this, but I intend to try." He kissed her hand and took his leave of the Rolfes.

Returning to his hut, lost in his thoughts, he scarcely noticed the sloop coming into the Rolfes' mooring.

Competition

The first Becky knew of the visitor was Jane's call and wave to recall her from John's experimental tobacco field. "Becky, there is a gentleman to see you."

It could not be D'Arcy returning so soon. Who?

Flushed and warm from the spring sun, she entered the great room, a combination of living and dining rooms.

"Becky, this is Captain William Tucker, the burgess of Kecoughtan. My cousin, Rebecca Cox. Will you both be seated. As I recall, William, you find John's ale quite refreshing. May I fetch you some?"

"Thank you, Jane, I would welcome it. Miss Cox, would you like this seat by the wind hole? It was my favorite when I stayed here last summer while the assembly was in session."

And so they conversed until Jane rejoined them.

"My plantation is quite a distance from here. The land is well situated. It was with high hopes that my wife, Alice, and I moved from Jamestown three years ago. Our tobacco crop prospered. A son, Timothy, was born, and we took on two indentured servants, a man and his wife, to help us indoors and outside.

"All went well until a few months ago. Alice gave birth to little Margaret. At first Alice seemed to be recovering her strength, but a fever began. We could find no way…That was three months ago, Miss Cox."

"This happened since you came here for the assembly?"

"Yes, that is so. I know it is almost unseemly to present myself to you so soon after Alice's…Alice's death. You must think me callous to seek another wife so soon. But necessity, my dear, here on the plantations is making early remarriage a common practice. I cut a poor figure in the midst of these rollicking young men, and realize this all too well!

"Miss Cox, I saw you for the first time when you came into the church on the day you landed. You looked fresh and lovely, full of life and laughter.

I knew then that if I were to stand any chance to win your hand, I should speak soon. Even then a bumpkin had you by the arm!"

Jane smiled behind her fan, for Becky showed that she deeply resented this remark.

"We need gaiety in our home again. Children need it as much as food and drink. We need the peace and order that a woman brings with her. Will you consider this a proposal of marriage, my dear? The little children and I have great need of you."

Becky murmured something, and whatever it was she could never recall later. She was honored. She would consider. Tears were stinging her eyelids, and she felt numb and saddened.

John Rolfe joined them. His face looked pale and the lines in it showed deeply. "Ho, William, my good friend! Your handclasp cheers me greatly this day."

"I had hoped to see you before departing, John. My mission here has just now been stated to your fair houseguest. May she give it most careful consideration!"

"Ah, this brace of ships with their attractive cargo has been the cause of your leaving Kecoughtan?"

"And a prompt return is now in order, for the boy is tearful when I am away. The infant is unaware of the sadness around her."

"I think of you often, and my heart bleeds for your bereavement, as my letter could not fully convey to you. Can you bear a further burden?"

"With God's help. Would that I had set sail a quarter hour since!"

"Nay, it is the greatest of good fortune that you may bear this news to your borough. Governor Yeardley has just received rumors of further Indian unrest. How much do you know? On the death of Powhatan in 1618, his chief of staff became his successor as the head of his confederacy. All of the village chiefs under Powhatan were called his brothers, or sisters, but the most powerful was his chief of staff, Opechancanough. Blood brother or no, he has an ambition to use his power, as well as a clarion call to leadership that we never saw in Powhatan."

"Do you suppose, John, that your marriage, if you will excuse me, Jane, to Pocahontas deterred Powhatan from making war on the colony? And even after her death, he kept the peace in her memory?"

"It is very likely that this is so. But now Opechancanough is under no such sentimental constraint. He burns with hatred that we have settled on the ancestral lands of the Algonquins. This is the latest news on his activity.

"As you may know, when a chief dies, his body is placed in an ossuary and guarded for a period of time. Then the bones are transferred to another of their ossuaries, and the time for this honor to Powhatan is soon to take place. We hear that they plan to gather in a large congregation at that time.

It is said that Opechancanough is much in evidence at their council meetings and speaks at length."

"What says Governor Yeardley to these rumors and bits of news?"

"This is his message that you must carry back at once to your township and to your neighbors. The governor urges that additional precautions be made all along the James River, and that the settlements be constantly on guard, ready for any aggressive action on the part of the Indians."

"He has made these recommendations for years. Will the people heed his warning and mount more guards? People do not like to believe such danger, nor do they choose to live with fear."

"I know not, William. All I can say is Godspeed, and do your best to alert the settlements as you proceed downriver."

"Now I must away if I am to deliver the message and reach my moorings ere nightfall. Farewell, my dear Miss Cox and Jane." Then Rolfe accompanied him to his sloop.

Background

To Becky it seemed a long time since she had strolled in the tobacco field. The distinguished, dark-haired stranger with his burden of grief had moved her to pity. He was more appealing than she wished to admit. His gentlemanly bearing and graceful manners seemed to linger still in the Rolfes' great room. She marveled at the social graces she had found in this small outpost of England in this savage land—this wilderness.

Savage. The word made her heart beat faster. Were the Indians going to rise up against the colony? Even the governor was asking for more defenses and a warning system.

John Rolfe now rejoined his ladies. He addressed himself to his friend's proposal. "I have known William Tucker for years. Naturally he is lacking in vivacity now, but his natural love of fun and laughter will return. He is a fine and capable man." Here John laid a bit too much emphasis on the word *capable* to suit Becky.

"Now, if you will forgive me, Jane my love, I must tell Becky how I myself have twice been a widower. It was just ten years ago that the *Sea Venture* headed a small fleet bound for Jamestown. Aboard were Lieutenant Governor Sir Thomas Gates and Admiral Sir George Somers. George Yeardley came as captain of the militia. I was aboard with my wife. Jane's father also was on the ship, but his wife and young Jane here were aboard the *Blessing* with a few other women.

"We ran into a hurricane which dispersed the ships. Our *Sea Venture* shipwrecked off Bermuda, while the *Blessing* was able to reach Jamestown in safety."

"Our arrival without the supplies that were aboard the other ship caused great suffering that winter," added Jane sadly. "We also were heartsick in thinking the ship and Father were lost."

"My father took me to London," said Becky, "and we saw *The Tempest*, the beautiful play that Shakespeare wrote after he heard of your misadventure."

"I know that he concocted some romantic nonsense from the affair. God is my witness, ladies, that we had something else to do than chase an Ariel spirit from tree to tree: My wife died there with our newborn infant. We men constructed two pinnaces, the *Deliverance* of 80 tons and the *Patience* of 30 tons burden to take us to the Virginia coast.

"Had we but reached here earlier, without reason of detainment by shipwreck, we might indeed have spared Jamestown that terrible winter of 1609 and 1610. We still call that the starving time. Did you hear, Becky, that there were 500 colonists in the fall, but by spring only 60 still lived? They were a sorry sight, I can take oath on that."

"Were you in Jamestown, Jane?"

"No, Becky, we were spread out among the settlements. We were short of food, but not so desperate as they were here."

"There we were," continued John, "just having rescued ourselves from shipwreck to arrive in such a terrible situation. Do you wonder that we decided to give it up and go home? But we had not cleared Chesapeake Bay before we met Lord De La Warr's fleet bravely advancing in a brisk wind. He breathed fire when he saw what we were up to! He persuaded us to return. Some of us cursed, and some of us cried, but return we did and settled this colony!"

"Reverend Buck arrived on the ship with Governor De La Warr," Jane added. "With his vigor and constant encouragement he earned the respect of us all. He was well chosen to be the head of our Episcopal Church.

"I do not fully understand the name. I thought we are part of the Church of England, John."

"True, we are. When the Church of England was brought to the colonies in Bermuda, Ireland, and Virginia, it was then called the Episcopal Church. It is still the same Protestant Church that Henry VIII began with himself at the head. Do you know how this came about, Becky?"

"Yes, Henry petitioned the pope in Rome to be allowed to divorce his wife, Catherine of Aragon. Henry claimed that he was wed to Catherine illegally, for she had been the widow of his brother, Arthur. It had been his father's deathbed wish that Henry marry her, so he did. Only one of their five children had lived: a daughter, Mary. Now he wanted to marry Anne Boleyn in the hope of having a son to succeed him."

"I wonder," remarked Jane, "what Queen Isabella and King Ferdinand would have said to this unkind treatment of their daughter. By then they had both died."

"You ladies seem to know Henry's history very well."

"He was an interesting king," smiled Becky.

"That he was. How did you become so well informed?"

"My father, being a merchant, had great respect for King Henry because he ordered so many ships built. Later on in Elizabeth's reign, this fleet and a great storm made it possible for England to defeat Spanish sea power. Were you alive when the Spanish Armada sailed to challenge England?"

"Three years old was I in that year 1588."

"It was Father who taught me what Henry had done to make our sea power strong enough to settle colonies in the New World in defiance of Spain. He stirred in me a sense of adventure that made me decide to come here after his death."

"And yet you have not mentioned Henry's personal history that people associate with him at once—the sensational succession of his six wives."

"Oh yes, I know about his one Jane, two Annes, and three Catherine's," smiled Becky, "but Father made sure I understood what he had done for the English navy."

"What I remember best," added Jane, "is that Pope Clement VII refused to allow him to divorce Queen Catherine. Then Henry declared that he would no longer belong to the Catholic Church of Rome! The pope excommunicated him! Henry set up the Church of England under his own leadership. Because he had protested against the pope's authority, the Church of England is a Protestant Church of the Christian faith."

"Now I understand that the Protestant Church of England here in Virginia is the Episcopal Church."

Just as John placed another log on the fire, a little high-pitched pleading cry was heard. Jane let in the cat, which went at once to John and jumped into his lap. "Well, Caligula, were you feeling lonely out there?"

"Caligula! What a name for a cat! Wherever did you get it?" laughed Becky.

"When Jane first saw these little white paws, she suggested the plebeian name of Boots. Since Caligula means *little boots*, we gave this noble creature the name of the Roman emperor. You see, cats are more than endearing pets here. They protect our grain storage as well as our homes from rats and mice. So you deserve an honorable name, do you not, Caligula?" John stroked his animal's head with a gentle hand.

"What did you yourself do after Lord De La Warr led the settlers back?" asked Becky, hoping that John would tell her more of his fascinating life story.

"Well, while Governor De La Warr and his Lieutenant Governor Gates were organizing the colony and expanding it, I was asked to experiment with the native tobacco and some tobacco seeds from the West Indies. This was on what is now my plantation near Henrico. My 1613 crop proved much to the liking of the people back in England, as well as here. Meanwhile, the young daughter of Powhatan, his favorite child Pocahontas, had been seized and taken to the fort by Captain Argall."

"Was that the same man who became governor, Sir George's good friend, the one little Argoll was named for? Why did he capture Pocahontas?" John laughed at Becky's excited questions.

"The same, the same! Ah, what a piece of treachery it was by bribing the Indians with a pot of copper that he got Pocahontas into his hands! Now why? The little Indian maid was a hostage to ensure peace between the colonists and her people. It was Gates' proposal that she be sent up to Henrico to the School for Indian Children for instruction in Christianity. It was there that I fell in love with her. She became a Christian when Reverend Buck baptized her, and she chose for her new, Christian name... Rebecca!"

Here he smiled warmly at Becky. "We were married in 1614. My tobacco was a huge success. Every colonist was planting it in every patch of land."

"Why did tobacco become a more profitable crop than wheat or some other food crop?"

"Tobacco is native to this soil, so it grows well. More can be grown on an acre than any crop we grow for food. One man can grow a crop of tobacco worth six times as much as the wheat he might raise. With few people to work in the fields, this is important."

"And the Virginia Company must have been delighted to have a profit coming in at last from their venture," nodded Becky.

"Spoken like a merchant's daughter!" approved John.

"Do the fields have to be dug up completely to plant it?"

"No, our tobacco is planted in hills, like corn, so the entire area need not be spaded. We plant it as do the Indians."

"And you had advice close at hand. Do you want to tell me what happened to Rebecca?"

"After our son, Thomas, was born, I was determined to take my family to England. My Indian princess was a tremendous favorite over there, and we even had her portrait painted. Later on she became homesick and pleaded to return to Virginia. I made arrangements, and we were ready to board ship. She was too ill to be moved by then, and she died there in port. My brother had taken a great fancy to Thomas, so I left him in loving hands. He is there now and doing well in his studies.

"Not long ago," he continued, "Jane did me the honor of becoming my wife. Her tranquility is making me very happy. My hope is that our friend, William Tucker, will be as fortunate."

Startled, Becky was brought back to the present.

"He could offer you a fine life, Becky," mused John, sending up a pretty spiral of smoke. "He has servants and broad, fertile acres. He manages his affairs well. You may visit him if you wish before you decide how to answer his proposal. Jane or I would gladly accompany you to Kecoughtan."

"I pity him. The idea of those motherless babies makes me feel needed, but I love D'Arcy. He needs me too, even more than William. He wants to bring literacy to this colony, just as you want to bring prosperity. Please help us!"

"It seems that your mind is made up, Cousin," said Jane softly. "There is a kind of magic in the air when you two are together. Then too, perhaps I am more than a little selfish in wanting you nearer than Kecoughtan."

"Ah, you women! There is the bell for evening prayers. Let us pray on these matters." And John Rolfe tapped the tobacco from his pipe.

"In a few more moments I shall again see D'Arcy," thought Becky, and her heart gave a lively little leap.

The Question

Becky woke the next morning with a sense of distress. Her bed clothing was tangled, her pillow wet with tears. Her head throbbed. "I remember now. Indians! They were making a surprise attack! It was terrifying." she recalled.

She dressed quickly and joined the Rolfes for church. She regained her composure with the help of Reverend Buck's morning message, a glimpse of D'Arcy, and then a good meal in the Rolfes' pleasant great room. The goat's milk tasted delicious after those long weeks of monotonous sea fare, as did the fresh egg. She was becoming fond of the gritty-textured cornbread with its sweet aroma and hearty flavor.

"What are the servants doing today?" she wondered. Taking her knitting to keep her hands busy, she wandered about this town property, where the Rolfes moved from their plantations when he had duties as councilman. They were located just outside the fort in New Towne.

Now she watched the indentured servants tending a small bed of experimental tobacco plants, preparing a fire in the smoke house to cure a new batch of hams and bacon, feeding hens, and here was Jane's mother, her own Aunt Jane Pierce. "Good morning, Aunt Jane. You are gardening early."

"And a good day to you, my child. John asked the other day if he could have one of my fig trees. I have just set this one that should grow nicely. Now I suppose the governor will want one as well. That man enjoys all sorts of fruit growing. I myself specialize in figs. There!" she said, giving the soil another gourdful of water. "I hope it grows well. Would you like to join me to talk with Jane?"

"I would gladly…except that a visitor is arriving."

"That is your young swain, D'Arcy, is it not? I may see you later, my dear." Aunt Jane hurried off to the house.

D'Arcy entered the garden with eager steps. He had never looked so handsome, she thought, with his brown hair neatly tied at the back of his neck. His long-sleeved white shirt looked fresh and comfortable this warm forenoon. The brown leather breeches ended with a band below the knee. Simple hose showed between the breeches and the sturdy buckled shoes, which completed the practical male attire. Becky looked up into his lively blue eyes and returned his smile. He seemed to radiate new confidence in himself.

"Nobody told me that you can knit," he began. "What other housewifely arts can you practice for my welfare?"

"I am learning to make a savory pitch-piney sauce to dress fowl."

"Just so you do not use it on fish."

"Pitch on perch? Why, I would never do such a thing! But I can hardly wait to try my hand at tarred turkey in a wattle-and-daub pastry."

"And I was so hoping that eventually we could invite the Rolfes to take a meal with us." The corners of his mouth turned down into a tragic-comic expression that made her laugh.

"Come into the house, D'Arcy, do!" The servants had overheard quite enough.

Becky led the way to the great room, where they found Jane and John standing by the open doorway. Three handsome Indian baskets full of D'Arcy's belongings stood by his sea chest.

"Jane, he does not care for my meal planning, with all that we need as close as the nearest swamp," pouted Becky with a mischievous glance.

"Such humble fare is beneath the dignity of an instructor's household."

"Oh, D'Arcy!"

"This morning, sir," he said turning to John Rolfe, "I met with the governor and Lady Temperance. She plans to do some tutoring of her own children and a few others. I shall work with her, instructing children in Jamestown, like Jamie, when they can be spared from other duties. I shall continue to be a public scribe for those who cannot write, and to assist Secretary Pory as clerk as needed, particularly during meetings of the House of Burgesses."

"And I?"

"We plan to stand you in a wine vat, come fall, and you can dance on the grape harvest," John announced with a twinkle in his eye.

"In my bare feet? Like they do in Italy?"

"And your skirts tucked up," grinned John.

"And purple juice to your knees," laughed Jane.

"Actually we do make a very good wine," sighed John. "If only we could ship it to England without so much spoilage, we could make a good profit there."

"What do you think of these plans, Becky?" asked Jane.

"Surely D'Arcy is not going to rush me out your door without…some sort of…ceremony…?"

"Oh, I have thought of that. I plan to thank your host and hostess very kindly for their hospitality to you and their considerable service to me," beamed D'Arcy, pretending not to understand her at all.

"Anything else?" Was her lip quivering?

"Yes," and he tenderly took her hand. "Jane and John have offered to witness our wedding this afternoon. Reverend Buck said he would be happy to perform our ceremony. He is getting quite hoarse after these two weeks of wed…."

"Oh!" sobbed Becky, bursting into tears.

Jane and John looked at each other with raised eyebrows. It had seemed to them that all of this maid's troubles were over.

"Aw, come now," murmured D'Arcy, folding his arms gently around her until she was held close to his best white shirt. "Have we teased you too much? What is the matter?"

"You have never asked me to marry you! Not properly!"

Jane and John Rolfe dissolved into helpless laughter. Her lilting peals and his hearty bass rolled through the open door into the fair May morning.

D'Arcy Takes a Wife

Apparently Becky's problem was solved to her complete satisfaction.

"A lovelier bride has surely never before stood in this church," D'Arcy thought, and he felt tears come to his eyes. "It is women who weep at weddings," he told himself sternly, and stole a glance at John Rolfe, who had just given away the bride. There were tears on his cheek.

"Are his thoughts for his first wife, buried with their baby girl in Bermuda?" wondered D'Arcy. "Or for Pocahontas, who stood at this altar so long ago? Perhaps they are tears of gratitude in having wed Jane."

Their matron of honor, Jane, was smiling tenderly at Becky. Aunt Jane and Captain Pierce had joined them, as had Jamie and a few other friends.

Through it all D'Arcy must have made the expected responses, for suddenly there was the good pastor smiling upon him and saying, "I now pronounce you man and wife."

For the next two days they remained at the Rolfes' while setting in order the little house that had been allotted to them. D'Arcy built shelves and rearranged furnishings for greater convenience.

Becky could hear the chunk, chunk, chunk of the firewood that he was tiering outside. She was opening parcels of her dishes, pots, pans, linens, blankets, and all the things she had so carefully packed in Liverpool. When she had wrapped these plates, she had been wishing, dreaming, and wondering about the man who would become her husband across the sea.

She sat back on her heels for a moment as the scene came back—the very moment when she had made up her mind to leave.

The funeral was over. Her beloved father had after all these years finally been reunited with her mother, and they lay in the country churchyard. Becky walked with her pregnant sister Margaret to the nearby vicarage. The four little nieces and nephews were all racing about, competing for attention, for their lives had been sorely disrupted by the death of their grandfather. The house was in utmost disorder.

"Becky, come and live with us," Margaret offered lovingly. "You cannot live alone in that great house at Liverpool. Father's partner will manage the trade with the Normandy ports. What is there for you there now?"

Becky had thought of the great house, so quiet now that the bustling merchant was gone along with his robust laughter and the constant coming and going of his peers in the overseas trade. She had thought how dreadful it would be on those nights when the dank cold fog swirled in from the sea to envelop the silent old stone house above the dockyards.

And yet, if she joined the household of Margaret and the vicar, there would be the endless care of the children. Bless her, Margaret could surely use two more hands, especially with another baby soon to arrive. But once she had accepted their hospitality, could she ever break away?

It would be better not to move in at all—better to go away and make a new life altogether. It would be better to pay off Father's gambling debts, then join the brides' ships bound for the colony in Virginia!

Now here she was, placing her belongings in her new home with the greatest happiness she had ever known, setting up her household for her handsome young husband. Surely she was the luckiest bride on either of the two ships!

D'Arcy brought in his Indian baskets. Becky and he stood hand in hand admiring the effect they made in their great room. These baskets increased their storage, and they looked handsome. Becky was sure nobody else had anything quite like them. D'Arcy had traded for them because they were such fine samples of the Indians' skill in basket weaving, not because they were dusty or sticky containers for trade goods.

"What do you think of my dowry?" he asked. And they laughed.

"How did you know what to bring over here?" she asked as he placed his sea chest beside the hearth as a seat and another place to store articles.

"The Virginia Company either supplied a man, or gave him a list of 'necessaries.' I provided my own, for my father proved both generous and encouraging in my undertaking. Here is my Monmouth cap," he said opening the chest. "Sailors and soldiers wear these brimless caps. Here are the three falling bands. These large white collars are far more comfortable than the stiff ruff worn in Elizabeth's reign."

"I have heard that those ruffs were the fashion because the queen had a skin disease, and she wore the ruff to conceal her neck, even up to her chin. How uncomfortable!"

"All true. Here are the three shirts, waistcoat, suit of cloth, suit of frieze...see what a thick woolen cloth this is. Feel it. And shaggy on the outside to keep out the damp cold and winds of winter. Here are the canvas work clothes, made chiefly of flax, and I have worn out some of my supply already. Three pairs of Irish stockings and three pairs of extra shoes. We have to be careful to keep them dry or they will mildew in this climate, so we keep them well wrapped in cloth. The garters are here, and here you see my last pair of knit socks.

"So! That is why you married me! You were down to your last pair of socks!"

"That was only the first reason," he drew her close for a little kiss. "The second is that I need a good woman to wash my falling bands clean and white," he grinned as she beat him about his head with the falling bands. "Careful there! They have to last a good while, you know. To finish this off, we had to bring canvas sheets and a canvas tick to fill with straw over here. This heavy rug, or blanket as you will, was very welcome on those blustery nights at sea. You will welcome it when the weather is chill in the fall, winter, and early spring."

"Did you have to contribute to the food stores?"

"My share for supplying the ship was eight bushels each of wheat meal and oatmeal, two bushels of peas, a gallon each of wine and oil, and two gallons of vinegar. Any extra rations after our voyage went to the cooks for community meals."

"You once mentioned bringing armor."

"Yes, indeed. My brother helped me procure a suit of armor. Then I needed a sword, belt, and bandoleer; musket and pistol; 20 pounds of powder and 60 of shot; and plenty of lead goose shot. All of this is in the guard house to be used as needed."

Becky learned quickly how to care for their two-room house. She cooked over a little fireplace and strewed rushes over the dirt floor. They had a common wattle-and-daub hut, set back from the main thoroughfare, which ran the length of the settlement. It was a small and cozy home. With summer heat coming, it was a fine place to live, but she wondered if they would have ways to make it warmer for the winter.

Town Talk

D'Arcy was away most of the day training new men in the Swamp, helping Mr. Pory, or writing letters as public scribe for a fee. Then he would spend some time with Jamie and some new boys on reading and writing lessons. This was proving to be a most interesting venture, for as they learned, D'Arcy was learning how to teach more effectively.

It was Jamie who kept him informed of what was going on since the maidens came. Today he was as full of news as a town crier. "Have you heard about the sergeant of the guard's affair?"

"The sergeant? That gruff old goat! None of them would surely consider that grumpy, sour-faced old soldier!"

"Then why were there two maidens competing for him? I ask you, two now!"

"Jamie, you jest."

"The first is a plump maid with a big nose and a loud laugh. That she can find so much to laugh about has your sergeant that interested." And Jamie winked.

"All this is causing you to grow up altogether too fast," sputtered D'Arcy. "Now what is the other like?"

"Now a more opposite kind of girl would be hard to find, I'm thinking. She is a tiny slip of a thing, all pale of hair and eyes light blue. It must be that she looks so defenseless that the sergeant feels like he should protect her, as I see it."

"I cannot imagine him with either."

"Yet it came to a contest between them, and that settled it."

"He has already decided on one? What happened, lad?"

"The plump one was feeling jealous when she sat at table near her rival. And her manners were shocking bad. She snatched away the portion that the pale maid would have had, saying, 'The pine tree smell has made me hungry,' to explain her act. The little one has spirit. She emptied the other's trencher into another as quick as a squirrel. Then she plunked herself down beside the sergeant, seeking his protection. He laughed like none of us had ever heard him laugh before. When he'd caught his breath, he turned to the lass and said for all to hear, "Ye've won your place at my side fair enough! Will you go with me to the Reverend Buck, come the morrow?"

"Well, I never! And Dickin, I hear, has a fine lass."

"That she is, and she rarely stops talking. With Dickin's love of stories, it makes you wonder who listens!"

"Rodney Gale has found a wife—Becky's friend on the ship. Have you met her?"

"Aye, Mary is her name, so we call her Merrie Gale. She is friendly to me for I remind her of a younger brother, she says. In many ways Rodney is fortunate, but I sometimes feel a bit sorry for him. I feel bad about that, her being so kind to me."

"What is distressing you?"

"Marrie Gale is the homeliest of all the maidens who came over on the two ships."

"Well now, you are becoming something of an observer in these matters. It will be very entertaining one day to watch you select a wife."

"You are laughing at me. There is many a lonely year for me before I will have a home and family of my own. It is lonelier now that you men are setting up your homes and moving from the fort. It makes me feel younger than ever. Everything has been changing since the brides' ships came."

"Yes, I have been aware of this. As we have met for your lessons, I have seen how the changes have affected you. Since the founding, changes take place rapidly. There will be those that benefit you too, all in good time.

"May I compliment you on your improving speech, young man? Your *ing* endings are ringing like a bell. Now let me hear you read your passage. Begin here."

Hot and Muggy

How it had begun neither of them knew. But it had led to his jutting out his jaw at his stubborn little wife. She had stamped her foot hard enough to make the dust rise through the rushes from the dirt floor. He had stormed out angry and hurt. She watched him stride up the lane.

She could almost see her perfect husband toppling off the pedestal where she had placed and adored him. She imagined him as a marble statue, toppled, broken into common dust.

"However does he manage to get about on those feet of clay?" she asked the cat with a nasty little sneer in her voice, her hands on her hips. Then Becky began to cry because she had been so awful to D'Arcy. Now he would hate her all day. Maybe forever!

She had never felt so HOT! And the day had hardly begun!

"Do we have to wear all these layers of clothes, even in summer?" she demanded of the cat, angrily shaking her voluminous skirt.

But the cat only looked down his nose at her and seemed to say, "You should be wearing a fur-r-r coat, my dear-r-r."

She scooped up her distaff, spindle, and flax to take to visit Jane. Perhaps spinning thread would help to keep her mind off the discomfort of the warm, sticky morning.

"Come in and let us keep as cool as we can," sighed Jane, waving her little fan a moment before returning to her spinning wheel. "John tells me that Sir George intends to have a talk soon with D'Arcy."

The Appointment

"Becky, have you seen my doublet? Oh, here it is. I must meet with Sir George. He wishes to discuss some matter. Whatever happened to my…."

"You look quite elegant, and here is your hat. Jane and I tried to guess what this concerns."

"You know nothing more than this?"

"No. There will be a hot, tasty meal waiting for you."

"Ah, you are telling me to hurry home as you are as eager as I am to learn what the governor has on his mind."

With a kiss on her brow, he left his wife stroking the cat and telling it, "My husband is learning to understand me all too well. Now get down so I can stir the pease porridge."

Hardly had an hour passed when he came hurrying home.

"Becky, I have been asked…where are you? I've been asked to go with all of his company to Flowerdieu Plantation to help him with his records and as tutor to all the children, even little Argoll and Elizabeth as they become old enough. We are to have a home of our own as soon as he gets the whole plantation in operation. You should see how excited he is now that his plans are getting on, and he can settle all of his people there presently! His family, his personal and indentured servants, and…."

"And us! How happy I am for you! But poor Jamie."

"I have arranged for him to go as a cook's helper at the big house, Yeardley's residence, so that we can continue his schooling and befriend him.

"Now help me. I must list all the things we shall need. There will be more books and supplies to request my brother and sister to send out on the supply ships. Help me make a list of the things left behind that I shall need also."

And a new adventure began.

Up the James

The wind was rising and whitecaps curled the surface of the James River, dark and blue today. The sky had become overcast since they had set sail for Flowerdieu with all their worldly possessions.

"That looks like a bad storm coming," D'Arcy observed. "Even with Flowerdieu nearly in sight, perhaps we should go ashore at the next wharf to wait this thing out. What say you?" he asked the helmsman.

"We be too far past Smythe's Hundred to turn back. Martin's Brandon lies on the south bank, past a creek. Aye, we should make that ere the rain comes."

Fitful winds made handling the sail difficult. Rapidly the sky was darkening. The rising wind chilled Becky. They had not planned on cold weather for the short sail on a day that was extremely warm in Jamestown. Opposite the creek entrance, a screaming gale tore across the river, heeling over the sloop. It had not seemed necessary earlier to lower the sail, but suddenly the ship was in danger of being capsized or driven onto the shore. The men grappled with the rigging. Becky clutched the rail with all her might, while D'Arcy feared she might be hurt by the erratic motion of the small ship.

The current from the mouth of the creek now caught them and was turning them. The helmsman could not manage his rudder as another gust hit them broadside. The sloop skittered fiendishly and inevitably into the muddy bank.

"...With everything we own!" screamed Becky as the sloop scraped bottom and slid to a tilted stop.

They were safe, the craft undamaged. Rain came with huge, spattering drops, then ceased. A lull in the wind permitted them to clamber ashore, moor the sloop fast to a tree lest the wind veer around.

"This rain will hold off for a bit. Hurry!" somebody yelled.

Amid some small trees they frantically rigged a spare sail for shelter, and then the rain came again as a deluge.

Silently they huddled under the makeshift cover as grey rain and cold wind swept past them. It grew wetter and colder, grayer and darker as the storm swept southward. There was nothing to do but cower down, eager to be on their way, and wonder how long the storm would last. Afternoon was edging toward evening.

"If we can get the sloop afloat, we can make a dash for it, sir," said the helmsman at long last. "The wind be slackenin'. The worst be past and the colder weather movin' into Tidewater. Ye mackerel sky yistiddy shown a big change comin', did ye but note er."

"I did see that sky," replied D'Arcy, "and the next time I am sure to remember what it means! A fitting name that, with the clouds patterned like a mackerel's back. Let us be away."

Between showers they boarded. It was good to be on the move once more toward their destination. D'Arcy prepared a place for Becky to lie in the small sheltered area. He tucked a pad of canvas under her head for a pillow and placed his doublet over her shoulder. She was asleep before they tacked into the main stream.

At last Flowerdieu came into view. They reached the mooring just as the western sky became a beautiful sight of rose and gold with shadowy blue colors beyond the pines.

Sir George himself came down to the wharf to greet them. Lady Temperance was comforting Argoll, who had just had a painful fall, but would join them shortly.

"All afternoon we have watched for you," Sir George said, helping Becky ashore. "Jamie came up with my family for this two-week visit, and he has been very worried about you since the storm arose. However, the evening meal has been prepared, and you are invited to share the roasted venison."

"This is a warm welcome indeed, Sir George," sighed a weary Becky.

"And we accept with pleasure," added D'Arcy.

"Allow me to escort Becky to the house to rest, D'Arcy. I shall send servants to help offload your gear. All will be under your own roof before dark."

"Our house is finished?" asked Becky, coming to life.

"Nearly so. It is far enough along for you to move in."

"I think my fatigue just went away," announced Becky, as she stepped out briskly with her hand on Sir George's arm. The men laughed, and D'Arcy turned to the business of debarking.

It was a most pleasant supper. Jamie was delighted to serve the fine meal that he had helped to prepare. Lady Temperance and Becky had many subjects to converse about in establishing their households at Flowerdieu. The men exchanged smiles when it became apparent that their pretty wives were finding such a lot of things to talk and laugh about.

Little Argoll wanted to be the center of attention, for it was an uncommon evening that his father could spend with the family, free of distracting matters that needed his time. Argoll had been watching the great migration of birds moving south in the warm days of Indian summer. He especially liked the sight and sound of Canada geese. Finally he was permitted a last flight around the great room as he shouted, "Ca-wonk! Ca-wonk! Everybody honk so it sounds like the flock!"

"Ca-wonk, ca-wonk, ca-wonk!" With this finale, Sir George swooped up his noisy gosling and bore him away to the nursery.

Becky yawned behind a graceful motion of her hand, but D'Arcy rose, and as soon as the governor returned, they thanked the Yeardleys for the gracious welcome to Flowerdieu.

Jamie appeared to light their way to their own little house with a flaming pine torch. He had been there earlier, for a fire burned cheerily in the new fireplace, and enough had been unpacked so they could have a good night's sleep. He blushed when Becky thanked him with a kiss on the cheek. Then she retired to the second room and was soon fast asleep.

D'Arcy motioned Jamie to a seat by the fire. "How do you like this plantation and working for Sir George?"

"I enjoy being with this family. They are very kind to me, and the work is far easier than working for Cook in Jamestown. Part of my duty is to care for Argoll, a very lively and interesting little boy. Last August he was two years old, and now his mother insists that he start learning to count and to say his letters. He has a lot to learn to become a plantation owner some day, and his parents are starting his education early. I wish I had been this fortunate!"

"You are making excellent progress," encouraged D'Arcy, noting further improvement in his speech. "I am certain Lady Temperance insists that you speak correct English to him."

"Yes, indeed! She corrects me whenever I err, and I am very grateful to her, as I am to you, sir. When are you starting classes? There are several of us who are to attend them. Sir George says that we may have time for tutoring if we work hard and value the opportunity. Otherwise, he has plenty of labor for us. There will be two who will be mischievous and end back in the tobacco fields very soon, but a half dozen of us will study hard as long as you are permitted to teach us!"

"Tomorrow we begin," smiled a sleepy D'Arcy. Jamie rose.

"What a lucky day for me when I reached Virginia!" And Jamie took his leave, well content to have the Southalls once again a part of his daily life.

D'Arcy banked the fire and sat down to watch the little glowing coals. Home. New responsibilities. He felt proud that he had these obligations to Sir George, to Becky, to Jamie. "All this gives a man a stake in the future," he thought. Then he let their cat out, barred the door, and went to bed.

Flowerdieu

Flowerdieu was as lovely as its name. It was the tract of some 3,200 acres on the southern bank of the James, and Sir George, in a sentimental mood, had given it Lady Temperance's maiden name, Flowerdieu. He had dreamed of the day when he would be able to live there, free of a governor's responsibilities, to plant his tobacco fields, to spend more time with his family, and to enjoy country life.

How eagerly he was anticipating minding his personal affairs after all his years of service to the crown as a military officer, not to mention the past three as colonial governor! In November his successor would arrive to take over the newly built governor's house in Jamestown and to assume his official duties. Only two more months until then, in this autumn of 1621.

September

Becky watched the sails of the windmill turning, turning against the hot blue September sky. Workers were still setting up the millstones and gears, for this windmill was being built to grind the new crops of maize, wheat, and oats.

"The first windmill in the colony!" she thought, and felt a thrill of pride that D'Arcy had settled on a plantation where there were so many activities. Having made their move the past November, she was observing her first harvest season.

She was enjoying the penetrating smell of drying tobacco. The huge crop was cut leaf by leaf. Each stem was slit so that it could be threaded onto lines, suspended on drying racks. These racks were suspended in barns to dry. She had heard how the leaves used to be buried in straw to cure, but a shortage of cattle fodder had led to this new drying method. Each year tobacco was by far the major crop. The prosperity of the plantation and all of its people depended on the care with which it was raised, harvested, cured, pressed into hogsheads, and shipped to England. Becky drew a deep breath of the sweet air.

She strolled home past the kitchen gardens. Heaps of golden onions were drying in wide rows and giving off a most savory aroma in the hot sun. Here was promise of tasty food in the cold months ahead! There were plantings of garlic and mustard seed too, but she did not pass them, as she wished to watch indentured servants who were tumbling turnips out of the pale soil. Further off others were digging carrots. Parsnips would be left in the ground until spring, but on the breeze came the clean, sharp smell of newly-cut cabbages.

Standing tall and ripening were the fields of corn, the ears heavy with yellow kernels. Beans and pumpkins were grown among the cornstalks, Indian fashion, so that the fish, placed in the hills at planting time, had fertilized all three crops.

Becky could see a group of pigs snuffling about in a patch of woodland. Swine, adapting themselves easily to the New World, were becoming a valuable source of food, while requiring very little care. During the summer they grubbed out the roots of the swamp plant tuckahoe. Now in the woods they were seeking fruits, acorns, and other nuts, collectively called mast, which would quickly build up their weight before winter.

Some women were harvesting flax. The protesting bleating of sheep informed her that sheep were being sheared over a rise.

Good crops of wheat, oats, and peas were already gathered in. What a comfort to know that these good English staple foods were carefully stored! There should be plenty for the long months until next harvest time.

Becky went into her house to fetch a knife and strands of flax so that she could hang the fragrant plants of thyme, marjoram, and sage about the kitchen end of their great room. With that finished, she decided, "I do believe that I shall harvest my lavender this afternoon."

Carefully she picked the long dry stems with their bell-shaped seedpods. She found a shady spot. There she gently rattled each dry stem against the side of the bowl in her lap to save the pleasantly pungent seeds.

Was there ever such a drowsy afternoon? Such peace?

In the distance the sail of the windmill turned and turned against the hot blue September sky.

She watched D'Arcy coming toward her from the big house, and as he drew nearer, she made up her mind. "What are you doing out here?" he called.

"It is the perfect day for harvesting the herbs," she returned.

Dropping down beside her in the shade, he grinned and observed, "You are the very picture of a prudent housewife with your herb gathering. What a marvelous day it is!"

"This plantation is a scene of bountiful harvests today, D'Arcy. It is a splendid place to make our home and welcome our little child to this world." He laughed and gave her a kiss.

"I have been wondering when you would tell me about this."

The New Governor

Lady Temperance had many words of an unofficial nature to say to Sir George, and he discovered an eloquence that he had not realized she possessed. She had in truth worked very hard to prepare the governor's house for her successor. On November 16, 1621, Sir Francis Wyatt arrived and assumed duties as the new governor, but his Lady Margaret did not find it convenient to leave her social life in London.

So it was with some sense of relief that Sir George left the government in the hands of Sir Francis. He and Temperance could settle down permanently at Flowerdieu, to return at times to their comfortable town residence near Back River. Taking Reverend Buck with him, he now decided to visit his Flowerdieu lands for two weeks to see how all was progressing.

Reverend Buck was about to christen several babies who had been born to Yeardley's plantation people.

"Perhaps on his next visit," Becky whispered, "our baby will be here, waiting to be christened."

"I am sure he will come back before then. When is it we expect our young Englishman? Is it May?" asked D'Arcy.

"About then. What a long time to wait! What are you saying about a young Englishman? *My* baby is going to be a native Virginian!"

"Yes, a Virginian, but as English as we can keep him, or her, even if the Atlantic does separate us from England. It is a proud heritage we give this child, him, or her. We simply must find a temporary name for this coming child! We cannot possibly continue to say 'him or her' all winter!"

"I was wondering when you would suggest that," laughed Becky. "Remember our meeting on the *London Merchant*? You thought I was Hope, the last creature in Pandora's box. How would you like Hopeful for a name while we are expectant parents? We can choose a fine name when we see the child."

"Hopeful it is. Hopeful 'til May."

"Here come the rest of the people. Now let us pay close attention so that we shall know what to do at our christening, hopefully."

Nursery Stock

Winter came on. Sir George Yeardley had never seemed so happy. He took long walks on his beautiful land and dreamed of ways to make it prosper. One day he strolled with D'Arcy through a young orchard, pointing out the newly planted peach, pear, plum, and cherry trees. In other fields were his apple, quince, fig, and grape plantings.

"Think on it. What is it that every householder will want, no matter how small his holding, as the years go by?"

"Could you be thinking of fruit trees? Vines?"

"Confound it, man, of course! There will be continuous demands for fruits to consume in season. Most enjoyable food we know! Fruits can be dried, preserved, made into wine. And once planted, fruit stock will produce for years."

"There must be something apt on an apple that I should be quoting to you at this moment."

"Do be serious, D'Arcy. Would you believe that I have invested every pound of tobacco I can manage in this nursery stock, both in England and among local growers? I am using every bit of charm that I possess...ahem...to win gifts of figs, grape roots, cuttings, even promises of cuttings from my friends. I believe that I can make my fortune in these fruits here at Flowerdieu."

"How do you translate the name? It is so odd being part English and part French."

"Flowerdieu? Flower of God. God's Flower. Perhaps even Flower and God. I wonder if it was originally Fleur de Dieu. Any one of these expresses my feeling for this land that I hope somehow to hand on to all of my children. There is enough here for all—Law of Primogeniture or no."

"So Flowerdieu was a happy coincidence as a name for a nursery, and I refer, of course, to your well-stocked nursery of two as well as to these thriving orchards and vineyards."

"Enough!" roared the knight, amused, clapping his friend on the shoulder. "Shall we finish this tour by letting you sample the wine from my Jamestown vineyard? By the great horned spoon, that last quip of yours deserves a toast to our Flowerdieu! And we must surely offer another to your lady in her fruitful condition, eh?"

And this time they both laughed and laughed.

The Tutor

Because of Sir George's preoccupation with his fruit growing, he had moved his family to Flowerdieu. During the fall a separate building for the small school had been completed. Classes had been set up for the little children in the mornings and for the lads of Jamie's age in the afternoons.

Sir George was showing a lively interest in the progress of the pupils. Argoll especially was more cooperative and learning faster with this personal daily attention from his father. Now, at the end of lessons, Sir George had come to let the children show him what they had accomplished. As he looked at their slates or asked them to read him a line, a cozy fire burned brightly, and the little pupils seated around the big table were warm and comfortable. D'Arcy was a kind and inspired teacher. Both he and Lady Temperance were well pleased with their little school. This class had now ended for the day.

In this interim before the boys came for their instruction, Sir George settled himself by the fire and lit his pipe. D'Arcy gratefully relaxed across the hearth and enjoyed the small meal that Jamie brought him at this time. They fell into a lively discussion of Shakespeare's plays and quoted long passages to each other.

Each of them savored these stolen hours, for there were always tasks they could have been attending. Their mutual interests often led D'Arcy to read a poem or a passage from some well-loved book to prove a viewpoint. "Let us keep this love of books alive in the children, D'Arcy. Let not the demands of frontier living rob our people of our literary heritage!"

"This, Sir George, is my vowed intent."

"I sometimes wonder if I should return you to Jamestown to set up larger classes there, and perhaps assist Governor Wyatt with his papers. What think you of this?"

"The idea of leaving Flowerdieu would be painful, sir. This is a fair place to bring up our coming child. It is fresh and lovely, not hot and airless on summer days, as it is in the capitol. There is room here. Jamestown is overcrowded and offensive with the mingled smells of village wastes and close-living animals. Here the very drinking water has a cleaner taste. I think it would be best for us to stay here while our child is small. This rolling shore land makes Jamestown seem unbearable by comparison."

"And still you have not mentioned the daylong clamor and clatter of the city!" smiled Sir George, well pleased with D'Arcy's eloquent plea to remain where he was. "Very well, stay here if you are so well satisfied. I had no idea that you, and presumably your wife, are so fond of my land! My lady and I are well pleased with your tutorial success. But, you see, there are times when I wonder if a larger number should not be benefiting from your instruction."

"You are too flattering, but I thank you. You spoke of my fondness of your land. We younger sons of the landed gentry, as you are well aware, have a passion to possess land. Denied by the Law of Primogeniture from ever claiming a part of our fathers' estates, we yearn avidly for our own country tracts. The hope of one day holding land in our own names has induced many of us to cast our lot on emigration to this colony."

"How forcefully you speak to the subject! Still you yourself make no effort whatsoever to claim acreage for your family."

"I do not want the care and worry of land just now. I am no farmer, Sir George. It will take all the advice that you and that master tobacco grower, John Rolfe himself, can give if I am to grow my little crop next spring on the plot you have put at my disposal. Furthermore, I can still claim no more than one hundred acres."

"Best not to wait too long, D'Arcy, for good land all up and down the American coast will he rapidly claimed from now on. A little band of Separatists from the Church of England, who call themselves Pilgrims, settled a colony they call Plymouth up north in Massachusetts last December. We learned from a fishing vessel that they survived the winter with only half their number, but hope for a good harvest, come fall. That is the beginning there, and it will soon expand, I have no doubt, so close it is to the great cod fishing banks. Claim your land soon, my friend."

Mild Winter

D'Arcy had never known so promising a time. He and Becky were enjoying this surprisingly mild winter as they awaited the birth of their baby with mounting excitement.

The Yeardley children, together with those of the plantation families, met each morning to learn arithmetic operations as well as to practice writing and reading. D'Arcy knew that literacy would one day enable his pupils to manage local church and business affairs, and some might participate in the government of Virginia. Argoll would be master of this plantation if all went well.

How hard D'Arcy worked to see that they were accurate in their learning! How he searched his memory to recall how this first stage of instruction had been presented to him! He was constantly adapting new ways to make his teaching clearer and more important to young minds. There was so much he wished to impart to the children. There was so little time with his day divided between the two age groups.

At the end of the day Becky would be waiting with a delicious meal simmering, broiling, baking. Jamie had even more helpful hints to pass on about food preparation, now that he was a cook in the Yeardley household. Often they asked him to join them to share Becky's successes and occasional failures.

Jamie was making a habit lately of rising extra early in order to start their fire blazing and to begin their morning meal. Becky appreciated this extra help, especially now, and so did D'Arcy. With his interest in learning reawakened, D'Arcy often read late by the firelight. He was reading all of his own books again. He eagerly accepted the loan of Sir George's treasured volumes. Having requested more from his family, he watched hungrily for parcels of books as well as paper and other supplies for his school whenever a ship arrived downriver.

These days, when he gave it any thought at all, D'Arcy knew he was happy and felt fulfilled. Others needed him, and he was doing the work for which he was best fitted—the work he loved. And Becky was his delight, his love, his amusing friend and companion. His whole world whirled around her, and all that he was doing was for her benefit in one way or another. Becky. So beautiful in these days of approaching motherhood, she had a new glow to her complexion and a sparkle of pure happiness that touched his heart.

Life was so good to them just now. Would they be allowed to hold onto this season of gladness?

December. January. February. March.

By mid-March planting activities were well begun all over the colony.

The Indians had been friendly for a long time. Some of their children had been taken into the colonists' homes to learn English in order that they could be taught about Christ and become Christians. This had from the beginning been one of the purposes of settling the land of Virginia. Many Indians were welcome friends, and many brought into the settlements useable trade goods and foods new to them.

There were no restrictions on the Indians coming into the communities whenever they wished. Sir George agonized over this while he was in office as governor those three years. Some but not all of the councilmen were worried too, despite Opchancanough's repeated avowals of friendship. Still he was a new leader, a more dangerous man than Powhatan, and now in a position of authority. Some of the councilmen were encouraging the new governor, Sir Francis Wyatt, to urge that weapons be kept handy, day and night. At night, lock up!

The spring sun was warming the earth and evoking a fresh vital fragrance. There was much to do up and down the James as planting activities increased.

A limit on tobacco this spring was restricting each grower's crop. A grower could put in 1,000 plants for each person he fed and clothed. Each plant should have nine leaves to harvest. This procedure should yield 100 pounds of top-quality leaf per person. This was one of the last rulings Sir George had arranged with his councilmen before his governorship ended, and he was very proud of this plan. He hoped it would keep the market price of tobacco from dropping in England, as it had done the previous year.

So ran the thoughts of the colony in the spring days that grew warmer with the approach of Easter.

Massacre!

On the morning of March 22, 1622, D'Arcy woke to the lively chatter of birds. "Nesting and the laying of eggs. Little birds coming," he mused as he rolled out of bed and smiled down at his sleeping wife.

There was a slight noise outside the door. Jamie was coming to build up the fire. D'Arcy unbarred the door to the youth, who was prompt and wide awake asking, "How is Mrs. Southall this morning?"

"Still asleep. I know that she will enjoy the fire well started, for there is a cool nip in the air. Make her a cup of sassafras tea as a special treat."

"It is a strange morning. The early mists have a peculiar feel to them."

"How do they feel strange?"

"Nothing that I can put a name to."

"It is Good Friday, lad. I recall that from early childhood, I have felt a tremulous quality in this day, a time of fear and foreboding. Is it this way with you?"

"That must have been at the back of my mind. Here is her tea, steeping sweet as you please. I have a piece of warmed cornbread here to go with her tea."

"I shall take it to her. She may wish to sleep a while longer after taking this. Warm us more of the bread and cook the eggs as you will."

D'Arcy carried the food and drink to Becky, waking her with the gentle question, "Have some tea?"

"Tea? Am I sick?"

"I hope not! Here, have your little meal, and you may sleep on. I want to set out a few tobacco plants before it is time to begin class. I am setting out 3,000 plants, so you must do your part if we are to claim that third thousand this year."

"Surely Hopeful is going to mean more to you than 1,000 plants or tobacco! The tea is good. I'll have the bread and very happily go back to sleep. I am glad I do not have to rise yet. Thank Jamie for me, as this is tasty."

"The rest will do you good. And I shall drive away that noisy woodpecker when I go out. Sleep well, little mother." He kissed her brow and returned to the fireside.

The man and youth ate heartily of the good food. The sun would soon be up. Jamie left. D'Arcy set himself to planting the little tobacco plants. The sun was nearing the eighth hour. It would presently be time to give this up and go to the school. Was there time to prepare the soil for....

Indians! They came from nowhere! They carried celts!

A cold fear bristled the hair on the back of D'Arcy's neck. Dread washed over him—a terrible concern for his wife, sleeping, vulnerable, only a few yards away behind an unlocked door. What were they up to? They came on.

D'Arcy edged toward his door, to put himself between them and Becky. How silent they were in the way they moved! And fast! Some were cutting him off from the house. No way to reach Becky now! No way to warn her to get up and lower the heavy wooden latch...Others were coming at him straight on!

At least he had the iron hoe in his hand. It would match that stone axe for a swing or two. "Our Father, which art in heaven, hall...God, thy will be done!"

The leader was before him now. Their eyes met. A look of recognition passed between them. In spite of that expression of bloodlust, D'Arcy knew he had seen this man before and where. He could just grasp his meaning.

"You gave knife for baskets, not trading with greed and trickery. Your chief Yeardley has tried to be fair. We will not kill you, not burn your houses. We go. Other places we to attack." And suddenly they obeyed his whoop, and they were gone.

All was quiet except for his thumping heartbeats. Then horrible screaming and piercing cries came down the hill. Up there the Indians must have attacked before the leader had had time to collect all his warriors. Jamie!

D'Arcy, collecting himself, charged into the house to see if Becky had heard or seen any of this. She still slept. Now he dared not leave her. What if they returned? Whatever had happened up yonder?

"Mr. Southall, are ye safe?"

Jamie was coming, tearing down the path. D'Arcy raised the latching bar to let him in and lowered it promptly. "Oh, am I glad to see you! We are safe now, but what was that racket? Tell me quickly!" Now he took a good look at Jamie. So pale that his freckles looked odd, the young man was ill and shaken. To talk would do him good, and D'Arcy needed to know what was happening. "Come, tell me."

"Indians sprang out everywhere. No yells, just groups of them rushing down on the men in the fields. Some men were bent over their planting. They never knew what hit them. They never stood up again. Oh-h-h."

D'Arcy gathered the shaking youth in his arms and let him sob. He knew the terror that he himself had endured a few minutes...or was it hours?...

ago? But he had not witnessed the killing nor the stunned, hysterical reactions of survivors. Poor Jamie had seen it all. If ever Jamie needed his older-brother comfort, it was now.

"Stay here, Jamie. Bar the door after me. Open it only to one you know for certain. I may be needed out there. If Becky wakens...."

"D'Arcy, what is all this talking? Why are you still here? Is your school not yet started?"

"I am going out now to see if I am needed. Jamie will be with you. The worst is over, I am sure, or I would not leave you. When I return, I shall tell you about it." To Jamie he added softly, "Do not tell her this is an Indian uprising, nor about the deaths." Then he continued aloud, "I shall be back as soon as possible. Make more of the tea for you both." His voice broke. "I am glad you are here safe, my dear Jamie. Now bar this door after me."

Taking his musket, he rushed off to join the shocked group near the Yeardley house. The master himself was temporarily in Jamestown with his family. D'Arcy heard again of the brutal slayings of defenseless men in the fields. Some twenty of them, indentured servants mostly, had been under attack as the sun reached the hour of eight. Six were dead. How did it happen?

The still trembling people of Flowerdieu Plantation now gathered near the chapel. They avoided going inside. They did not want to be closed in anywhere.

"Opechancanough must be behind this!" began one. "Ever since that big gathering for the moving of Powhatan's bones to a new location, this uprising must have been planned. That was the last great meeting of the village chiefs of the old Powhatan confederacy. They had come from as far away as the Falls of the Potomac River."

"Lately they had all seemed friendly enough."

"Especially lately."

"Too friendly!"

"That is right, so we would not be so watchful."

"This allowed them to go everywhere in the colony."

"And at any time. Why one evening I came upon one after dark when I was going to the well."

"What a fool to be out after dark!"

"It was inside the palisade, I was!"

"How widespread is this attack, I wonder..."

"They did seem to be moving off to another settlement..."

"And why did they leave so suddenly?"

"They could have killed us all!" wailed a woman bursting into wild sobs.

"We had not taken the council's warning seriously enough, even here on the land of a councilman, which Sir George became after being governor."

"He warned us as governor, as councilman, and as our master, but that busy we were with the tobacco planting that we did not heed his advice."

"Who would move a musket along foot by foot as we plant or tend the rows?" a man angrily shouted.

"The Indians knew this—knew us well, they did—to plan it for this particular time!"

"Why so they did! With us so scattered upon the land, laborin' in earliest morn before the sun gets warm."

"Without our weapons."

"There is always so much else to tote about!"

"We had best be about the care of those poor lads yonder. Has Sir George ever said where the burial lot is to be extended?"

"Somebody is going to have to bear these tidings to him down at Jamestown."

"And the relatives in England must be told how the indentured service of these lads has so pitifully ended."

The overseer, Sergeant Fortescue, had noticed D'Arcy in the gathering. "Mr. Southall, will you depart as soon as you can to bear these sad tidings? And will you prepare the messages to the families of the deceased, sir? I dare not leave myself, lest the infidels return.

"Now I want every piece of weaponry brought here. We shall set up a watchman's schedule. These bodies are to be interred within the hour. The rest of you are to get on with your daily tasks. It will be for the best, for the sake of the children..."and his voice broke.

The people moved apart with heads bowed, lost in thought, there bodies leaden with grief and dread of what might yet befall them. But thanks to the overseer, each had a job to do and a destination.

"And to think that I used to wonder whatever delayed the Indians from doing this very thing!" marveled D'Arcy. He ducked his head against a rising wind and headed home to prepare for his mission. The early sun had gone. Rain came in spatters to sting his face.

"Good Friday. A dark, strange day of tension, terror, and violent death. Opechancanough. He must be nearly eighty now. He has been urging his people to do what is natural and understandable, I suppose. They are trying to stand off new people from coming in to take over their land, driving them into less desirable territory. Savages also have feelings for their homes."

He lowered his head still further against a pelting rain and picked his way across the muddy ground.

"In civilized countries we call it holy and justified war to fight for the homeland, to expel the invader. As colonists we regard this land as an opportunity for our people to expand and to grow in riches and power. Which of us has the better right to these beautiful Virginia peninsulas?

"How are the Yeardleys faring? And Jamestown?

"Is this uprising widespread?

"What can I tell Becky lest she suffer fear and shock? A baby due at a time like this! I never knew what safety meant! Will any of us live through this if all the Indians are on the warpath? My legs feel like wooden pegs."

D'Arcy reached his door and called to Jamie. Two blanched and worried faces begged silently for news. What should he tell them? He felt the unreal, unearthly mood of this day beating like a pulse in the silence.

They must have seen that his need was greater than their own. Becky took the initiative.

"Sit here by the fire. You are exhausted, my dear! Jamie has kept some tea hot, and you need it. Soaking wet too! Take off that garment or what a fever you will be having! This shawl will warm you."

The dear familiar sounds of a wife clucking like a mother hen over his little discomforts did more for him than the tea or shawl. He began to feel more normal. He could tell them now. They were both strong, brave people who could cope with his terrible news, but how to begin? His eyes moved to the three beautifully plaited baskets standing along the wall.

"Those baskets saved my life, and probably yours, Becky." Then he told them briefly of the morning's events and concluded, "So now you know what I must tell Sir George and write to the families of the dead. Fortescue has asked me to leave for Jamestown as soon as I can get ready."

Elsewhere

Meanwhile the Virginia colony was in a hysterical uproar. Boats of all sorts had begun rushing up and down the James from Kecoughtan to the falls. Jamestown was full of frantic men and boys. Governor Wyatt had immediately put Sir George in charge of all the militia, and all able-bodied men were to be called up in relays.

Only by the grace of God, they were saying over and over, did Jamestown call out her guardsmen in time on that terrible morning. An Indian boy, Chanco, had been secretly passed word of the planned uprising. He had been told to join in the attack on the settlements. This was to occur at sunrise on a day they had named upon every English community along the James.

Chanco had been living with the Pace family. He had only recently become a Christian. The poor youth, torn between his loyalty to his own people, to his new friends, and to his new faith, would have had an agonizing problem. What was he to do?

Should he keep quiet? Yes, that was best. It was not up to him to upset the long-laid plans of his Chief Opechancanough. But this decision brought him no peace.

He had been learning about that man. What was his name? Judas. Judas had betrayed Jesus. What happened after that had led to this Good Friday and then Easter time, which would be observed just two days away now. He, Chanco, was going to be another Judas. No matter what he decided, he would be a Judas! He would betray people whom he loved and respected if he kept silent or if he spoke out!

It was too much to keep inside him! Tell somebody! But hurry! Tell Mr. Pace! Hurry! There was not much time left anymore if the colonists were to save even their people closest to Jamestown! Hurry to Mr. Pace.

Mr. Pace carried the word to Jamestown. No time was lost in mounting a strong defense. The Indians found they were not willing to face the little evil cannons and deadly musket fire. Perhaps men who had stood many a long dull duty watch would welcome action.

Then rumors and reports from the plantations, hundreds, and townships began rushing in. Some places had been cruelly treated as the Indians, at long last feeling organized and strong under an old war chief, rose up to eliminate the people who had settled on their best lands. Some plantations had escaped with little bloodshed. It was otherwise at Falling Creek.

Falling Creek had been a most ambitious settlement. The East India Company in London had supplied some of the money to build its iron furnace. Profits from this furnace would be used to build a college at Henrico.

With a college in Virginia, the colony's young men, who finished their studies under their tutors in the future, would not need to make the long voyage back to England to complete their education.

In England the young men from America would he subject to such deadly illnesses as consumption (tuberculosis) and smallpox. Moreover, there was the excitement of English city life to lure them from ever returning to rural Virginia. The years that these sons would be away would seem long and full of dangers to families who wanted their young men to have university training at Cambridge or Oxford.

Falling Creek was to make the profits that would enable Virginia to build its own college: the first one in America.

But Falling Creek was the hardest hit of all the communities, although it did not lose the most people. Columns of smoke told the story. The iron furnace was destroyed. Homes were burned, and 27 people lay dead. The news reached Flowerdieu that day.

D'Arcy left off his preparations to sail to Jamestown. He led Becky to the fireside and, when she was comfortably seated, sat on the floor at her feet.

"We had been so sure that our sons would receive all the education they would need right here in Virginia! There is little chance now that a college can be financed and built by the time our sons are of college age.

"Then I must have been hoping for some type of teaching position at the college, not as one of the dons, for they would have been sent from England, but surely tutors would have been needed! This was the reason I have been reading lately.

"What a stupid, foolish prank! I never told you the whole story of why I was asked to leave Oxford after only one year. I lost my only chance then for a university education, but how very valuable that one year has become! It has made possible my work as clerk and tutor."

Becky could understand now why he was taking this news so badly. When she heard of his plans to participate in the college, she marveled at this farsighted man. How little she had known about him when they married! Such a fine person with so much to give to growing children! She looked down at his eyes full of hurt and bewilderment. He laid his head in her lap. Her fingers tenderly stroked the brown hair.

"D'Arcy, you still have your work in helping to prepare the reports that go back to London, particularly when the assembly meets. Being a tutor is an important job—more so than ever now when this kind of schooling will be the only sort available here for a long time to come. You will lay claim to your land too, even if those acres are not to lie near the proposed college. I see now that this was another reason for your delay in claiming our headrights. You will see fit to claim them in time."

"Some day," he whispered.

There was still worse news to come.

Downriver

Preparations were nearly complete for his departure, but D'Arcy hated to leave Becky. He dreaded telling Sir George of the trouble here. Was it only this morning that all this had happened?

Sergeant Fortescue called at the door, "Are you there, Mr. Southall?" D'Arcy unbarred the door and invited him to come in. "Since you are sailing down, sir, why do you not take your wife and your belongings with you? It would be one less person for me to be responsible for while you are away—more so if the Indians come back. She is related to the Rolfes and the Pierces, is she not? Surely they can take you in while you complete your business there. It may be that you may prefer to remain in Jamestown. What say you?"

"This is a good plan. Kindly send Jamie and some others to help us, and we can be on our way presently. Oh, and, Sergeant, do you know if Sir George has the full names of the dead servants, their indenture papers, names of parents, and home locations in England in his records up here or in Jamestown?"

"I have never seen them, so these papers must be in Jamestown. Imagine thinking of things like that at a time like this! Picked the right man for this job, so I did. I will have the latest news on the uprisings for you as the sloop sails. May you have a safe trip downriver, Madam, and good fortune with your babe." And he hurried away.

"This is a great relief to simply move you back to the capitol," D'Arcy stated. Then he fell to work, trying to keep pace with Becky, who was collecting their belongings.

"We can rest on the sloop. If we hurry, we can reach Jamestown before sunset, which seems downright necessary this day." Becky was gathering clothing into a blanket.

Gathering small things in his baskets, D'Arcy replied, "When was it I realized that you have a very good mind in that pretty little head?"

Jamie arrived with the boys in his class, and in no time they were all moving toward the dock, and the gear was being stowed. Fortescue gave them the latest news that Sir George would need to learn from this area. Good-byes were brief, and the sloop moved out into the current, the sail went up, and they were on their way. The combination of the current that carried them downriver to the fort and the favorable westerly wind in their sails promised a short trip this early afternoon.

This gentle sail proved to be a godsend. The sun came out, warm and beautiful. The air felt moist and gentle. The wooded shores with the pale green of the earliest spring foliage reminded Becky of the scenery in a favorite fairy tale. She thought, "There is magic in the old Irish tales that my old nurse used to tell me. The leprechauns lived in a land of emerald green with silver lakes and clear, golden sun that shone down on distant rain, and she said…."

"What are you thinking of? You seem a thousand miles away."

"Ireland. My old nurse told me Irish tales. Virginia has some of the beautiful atmosphere of her stories—the same stories that before long I shall be telling to Hopeful." Her hand felt warm in his.

"So much of that part of your life I have yet to hear. We still have so much to learn about each other's life before we met. Tell me more about you…as a little child this time."

"Very well. But we have all the rest of our lives to talk about these…."

The way his hand suddenly tightened about hers made her recall the morning. How much was left of "the rest of our lives"?

Would they ever be able to forget the Indian menace? Would life ever go back to normal? Would they ever laugh again?

Jane

Later that afternoon the sloop slid up to the Jamestown mooring, and D'Arcy helped his wife carefully ashore. How pleased he was that she was with him! Her color was better, and her eyes had regained their attractive sparkle. There was much to remind him of the maid whom he had escorted ashore on her arrival. Suddenly he had a splendid idea. He kissed her.

"D'Arcy! Such a way to behave! You will be put in the stocks forthwith!"

"It would not be the first time," he answered with the smile she loved. It was good to hear humor in his voice again. She would try again.

"To think that I am married to a common criminal! My poor babe!"

Ah, it was like old times with her light quips matching his. "Good for him to get a sordid start in life! Make him value any good luck coming his way."

"Poor, poor little Hopeless!" They exchanged a quick smile and began to gather their most immediate necessities.

Walking slowly up to the fort, they watched people hurrying with a sense of purpose that was new. The guardsmen were drilling in considerable number outside the palisade under the eye of Captain William Pierce. The sergeant of the guard looked younger, tougher. D'Arcy realized that he too was part of this militia. At any time he could be called away to serve with this small army, and leave Becky.

This infernal uprising!

"I shall take you to stay with your cousin Jane while I see Sir George and deliver Sergeant Fortescue's messages," he told her.

"That would suit me well. I am getting a bit tired although the sail was lovely. I am very grateful to Sergeant Fortescue for sending me with you."

"You look worlds better for the outing."

"Here we are. The house seems so quiet."

"Jane, are you there?" Becky called at the open door.

Her Aunt Jane Pierce, looking very pale and not at all her dynamic self, came to the door. "Pray enter, Becky, D'Arcy. Our Jane is resting. She will welcome your company. Sit you here while I fetch her."

Something was wrong. They exchanged glances as they awaited the arrival of Jane Rolfe. Presently she came, looking wan and fragile. "Becky and D'Arcy! How pleased I am…to see both of you."

"Jane, what has happened? We have had no news of you for so long."

"Let us go out to the garden, my dears. He loved it so…"

"Jane, what has happened?"

"Oh, yes. You have not heard. John…he had been very ill last winter. We despaired of his life, and he made a will. I asked Lady Temperance to witness it one day when he was very bad, and Sir George was away. It was after our new governor came. John fretted, being absent from the council at such a time. He so wanted to help Governor Wyatt get acquainted with the situation here in the colony. As the winter waned, his energy returned. By early March he was full of plans for planting his holdings. I knew he wished to be on hand when his people planted his fields. He wanted to make every seedling of the new hybrid count, especially with this new restriction on the number of plants. My father offered to oversee his fields downriver at Mulberry Point, the lands that they had developed together. My brother Thomas…had settled on our father's land."

Here Becky's aunt began to weep quietly.

"We learned a short while ago that Thomas, his wife, and little child have been killed by the Indians this morning. They were just here visiting on Palm Sunday."

"Oh, not Thomas!" exclaimed Becky, and she began to cry.

"You were telling us about John," said D'Arcy quietly.

"He chose to go to his lands upriver. I wanted to go with him, of course," Jane went on. "He would not hear of it. As a member of the council, he seemed more aware than most that the Indians were planning something quite widespread. The council could never learn when it might occur."

"He went to Bermuda Hundred without you earlier this month?" prompted D'Arcy.

"Yes. He planned to stay only a few days. There were to be so few tobacco plants for us and for our people this year. And he needed every pound of tobacco for debts in England, for Thomas's schooling, and for developing new tracts."

"Go on, Jane."

"This morning he was in the field. They all tell me that it was very sudden. They say he had no idea at all what hit him."

Becky was weeping quietly, but otherwise they were all silent for a time. D'Arcy spoke, "You have our deepest sympathy, Jane. I cannot believe that the Indians would do this to John Rolfe. For so long his friendship and his marriage to Pocahontas had made for friendly relations between the colonists and these Algonquians!"

"Do you not see, D'Arcy, that so much time has gone by—nearly ten years? The younger Indians, the warriors, probably did not recognize him, even on his own land! Then too, he had aged during his recent illness. I prefer to think that they simply did not know him. He was just another of the detested white men."

"So he is buried on his plantation, where he developed the tobacco industry to the benefit of the whole colony," said D'Arcy softly.

"And where he met Pocahontas," added Becky.

"For these reasons he belongs there," Jane said. "Oh, forgive me. I have not yet asked what brings you to Jamestown."

After hearing how Flowerdieu fared in the Indian assault, Jane sat up very straight. "I am so very glad that you have come. Please be my guests, for I have great need of your companionship. And now, Becky, you need rest while D'Arcy waits on Sir George with news of his plantation and the neighboring lands. My servants will bring up your baggage from the sloop."

"I shall return at the earliest possible time," D'Arcy assured them and departed. This day was changing all their lives.

On his way back toward the fort, D'Arcy learned that their neighbor, Samuel Maycock, a member of the governor's council, like John Rolfe, had been killed on his plantation upriver of Flowerdieu. But Merrie Gale and her Rodney were mostly on his mind. Here was new grief for Becky. The Gales had gone to Martin's Hundred, where the Indians had hit hard. The news was still spreading through the fort that 78 people had been killed there, including both of the Gales. Jamie too would be grieved by this news.
Having inquired as to the present whereabouts of Sir George, D'Arcy made his way along the pathway, crunchy with the shells of crushed oysters, to the Yeardley home on the Back River side of Jamestown Island. The ex-governor was taking a short rest. He had stayed by Governor Wyatt's side since early morning, receiving the reports and rumors as they came in.

Because he was the most experienced military man in Virginia, the governor was relying on him more and more with the passing of each terrible hour. Sir George looked pale, and shadows under his eyes told of the shocking news that he had been receiving all day.

"How good of you to come downriver at once, D'Arcy," was the warm greeting. "I have not as yet heard any word from Flowerdieu that I can rely upon. Come and sit here. Share this quiet moment with me, and tell me how we fared." And D'Arcy told him the whole story. It was the realization of the nightmare that had for years haunted the sleep of the man before him, D'Arcy knew, as he brought his report to an end.

"I am heartsick. Those indentured lads were promising citizens, every one, or I would not have chosen them. I must commend Sergeant Fortescue in charging you with informing their relatives. Likewise in dispatching you here with your wife and your household goods. Now the papers you require, in order to write your letters, are here. Lady Temperance will make them available to you in the morning."

"The messages will be ready for the next sailing," promised D'Arcy. "You may reach me at the Rolfes'…at Jane Rolfe's home," he painfully corrected himself. "Jane pleads with us to stay with her. We need her as much as she seems to require our company."

"Ah, I cannot yet believe that John is gone. My true friend all these years. And you have also heard of Jane's brother?" D'Arcy nodded. "Now comes the grim period of revenge and retribution, and I fail to see how it can be avoided. There is to be a meeting of the council with the governor early in the morning. But in the early afternoon, join me here, for we must make plans for you and the people at Flowerdieu."

"Until tomorrow then," agreed D'Arcy, and he departed, unwilling to take more of Yeardley's time than necessary, so weary did he appear.

He set his steps toward the fort. As yet only the nearest settlements, and a few of the distant ones, had reported what had happened with any certainty, but evidence was mounting alarmingly that the attack was widespread and devastating. Flowerdieu had come through with relatively little loss of life and damage to property compared with other places, but he was very glad he had moved Becky back here.

The March breeze caught up a swirl of dust along with the stench of pigs and necessary houses. Then there followed the smell of piney smoke from the tar-making fires in the Pitch and Tar Swamp. He had forgotten how strong these odors were as the weather grew warm!

"Dickin! Good it is to see you!" Here was a cheery soul to gladden his day.

"Why, Mr. Southall it is! A long time has it been since I last saw ye. How did you fare up there on the Yeardley lands?"

"Better than most today, even though we grieve for the six who were slain in the fields. When I came down to report to Sir George, I brought my wife and our possessions, for she is expecting our child soon. Jane Rolfe is taking us in. How is it with you?"

"Ah, that wife of mine is still the wonder! 'Tis a second babe we are lookin' for this fall. Our first is a boy, George, after our recent governor."

"Does Sir George know this? It would please him exceedingly to know that you did him this honor."

"Ye may tell him if ye like. It was many a fine thing he did when he held the power. And our first girl will be named for his lady, you may add, not for her ill-tempered successor! The likes of me oft speak o' the good days under Sir George Yeardley's rule."

"All this I shall tell him. What work are you now engaging in?

"Brewin' the ale I am with some grand equipment recently arrived. Would ye like to see m' brewery? 'Tis but a step over here. I have two apprentices I'm trainin', for 'tis a fair long period it takes to teach young fellers the knack o' turnin' out the beer and ale proper like. A brick oven we have now for dryin' our malt. The hops we grow on the fences by our own homes."

"What happens to a batch that does not turn out to your satisfaction? It goes sour, does it not?"

"That it does, but 'tis no waste, if that's what yer thinkin'. This is where our supply o' vinegar comes from. Whenever the beer or wine sours, we please the cooks with our fine vinegars."

"This is a good business you have going here, Dickin. You are a lucky man."

"Here, try a sample o' our wares ere ye depart. How does it compare wi' the first you tasted here? I recall ye sent a compliment by Jamie. How's the lad?"

"This is an excellent brew! Jamie is growing into a handsome youth. I am well pleased with his studies. Just between us, I think he would do well as a tutor. He has the patience I myself find lacking with the smallest pupils."

"A tutor's apprentice is it now?" Dickin laughed warmly. "This must be the first one in the colony! And ye're still teachin' him after all this time! That brings to mind a most serious matter to me. When are ye comin' back to Jamestown to teach the children here, like mine?"

"My plans are most uncertain, especially now."

"Fer what do ye think some o' us survived the starvin' time, and have been sweatin' out our lives over the menial work we could o' done more comfortably in England? I want m' Georgie and all the later sons to know how to read an' write. Yes, and maybe the girls too! Not grow up ignorant like the man ye see before ye, only good for the pourin' of his brews from one vat to the next! Somethin' better for the young ones! Promise me ye'll see that the children will have the chance we never had. See to that, Mr. Southall. 'Tis the reason ye failed in the work o' the common men, if I may speak plain, so ye could go on to higher things to the benefit uv us all!"

"Your words hearten me, my friend, and I shall think on them. You are right, for it is in teaching that I find a most satisfying occupation. Now I must return to my wife and her widowed cousin. We need her hospitality for a time, and it will be good for Jane Rolfe to be needed."

"'Tis a sad thing she has lost her man, for a fine and honorable one was John Rolfe. I'll be sendin' round some vinegar for the household and a bit o' ale for yourself."

"He will be sorely missed. Thank you, Dickin, for the talk as well as for the vinegar and ale. We'll talk again ere long."

Jane's Visitor

When Becky saw D'Arcy approaching the Rolfe house, she strolled out to meet him. They watched a visitor take leave of Jane by the door. "Do you know who that is?"

"He seems vaguely familiar, but I do not recall where I saw him."

"That is Burgess William Tucker paying his respects."

"Oh?"

"He and John were very good friends. He has a plantation at Kecoughtan, or Elizabeth City as it is now called. He is a widower with two small children."

"And how do you know so much about him?" asked a tight-voiced D'Arcy, ashamed of sounding as jealous as he felt.

"He once asked me to marry him."

"He did *what*? When was that? I thought I was the first man you found of interest."

"You were, my dear. It was while I was staying here with the Rolfes that he paid a visit and asked me to be the mother of his babies and to run his plantation."

"Nobody ever told me all this."

"No need. I had already met the man I wanted."

"Then why all the tears over my proposal?"

"I sometimes wonder too. I suppose it was simply the unsettled feeling girls have before the wedding. Or perhaps it was because he had proposed so beautifully, and you had just taken our marriage for granted."

"Humpf. Why are you telling me all this now?"

"I think that you should know about Captain Tucker in the event he asks Jane to be his wife."

"Jane! Now? Not so soon after John's death."

"If he does not, another will! He has recently lost his second wife. Yes, since he asked me, he has had another loss. Jane told me. Then too, Jane is a wealthy woman with all of John's land holdings, and some day her father's."

"Would you approve of this Tucker?"

"Oh, yes! He is a man whom John regarded very highly."

"Ah! So John urged you to marry him!"

Becky felt her face growing red. Now she had gone too far! "It was too late."

"How? " he growled.

"I simply told John that I love you," and Becky raised her eyes to his and smiled prettily.

D'Arcy had a strange weak feeling about his knees. He had come this close to losing her! How overwrought he would have been had he known that a rival with a couple of pathetic babies, and an established plantation moreover, had asked for her hand! A handsome devil too, he suddenly remembered, placing Tucker in the House of Burgesses. "Becky, you gave up being the mistress of a plantation!"

"But I am the wife of D'Arcy Southall."

A Talk with Yeardley

For a week Sir George was unable to keep his appointment with D'Arcy. Messengers with reports of killing and destruction continued to stun the residents of Jamestown. At some point Virginians stopped calling it the uprising. They now spoke of the Indian massacre.

Survivors, exhausted and shaken, seeking compassion as well as shelter and food, poured into the capitol. This was the situation when Sir George finally sent for D'Arcy.

Yeardley looked grey with fatigue, worry, and overwork. "Sit down, sit down," he began at once. "I must meet with Roger Smith directly, but first let me acquaint you with my plans.

"The death count from the massacre is nearing 350. In many places the people out on the plantations are giving it up, moving into or near Jamestown. We are overcrowded now, and conditions will only worsen. With the coming of this hot weather, the summer fevers will soon begin and more deaths can be expected. Do you follow me?"

"You have been painfully explicit, Sir George."

Both men were silent. Sir George's fingers drummed on a table. D'Arcy thought of the burdens that had been placed on this man in the past week.

The surviving members of the council, shocked to learn that four of their number had been massacred, had met with Governor Wyatt, who appointed Sir George as marshal of the military forces. The office of marshal had been vacant since the death of Marshal Neuce, who had died in late 1621 or early 1622 and had never been replaced by the Virginia Company. In no way could word have reached London, a new marshal appointed, and the new man reach the colony in time to forestall the massacre in March. A leaderless militia had given the wily Opechancanough a crucial advantage.

Out of necessity the governor and his council had been forced to fill the important and well-paying position of marshal. Profits from designated public land would pay this salary, but other thoughts now occupied Sir George.

"Once again we are under martial law, and war has been declared against the Indians. The army is every man and boy fit to bear arms, and we shall call them up in relays. Now they have put me in charge of relocating the people who have been withdrawn from the distant communities as well as those who have come in of their own accord, God help me. I am thinking of delegating this to John Pountiss, commander of Southampton Hundred, which was Smythe's Hundred under my management some hundred years ago, it seems."

"All this is too much for one man."

"At least, D'Arcy, the governor has given me complete freedom to set up the defenses I deem necessary against further harassment by enemies approaching by land…or water!

"My own people have to be provided for, and this responsibility I do not choose to delegate. What think you of this plan that concerns you? I shall move most of my people from Flowerdieu, where my rights to the land had never been made clear, to my lands on the Eastern Shore at Hungar's Creek."

"The Indians over there did not rise up, I hear."

"True, true! Debedeavon, the chief from whom I acquired 3,700 acres, would not join Opechancanough. What do you say to my good fortune in having a clear title to all that land?"

"I wish you the same luck in duck hunting."

Sir George roared with laughter for the first time in days. "You could not have known this, but the land is a peninsula you see, between the two forks of Hungar's Creek, and it is the very shape of a duck's bill!

"The question now is would you like to move your family over there? You would be tutor, keeper of the records, and a guardsman until you eventually wish to claim lands of your own."

"Do you accept Debedeavon's word that there will be no attack over there?"

"Not entirely. A strong palisade is to be built around the dwelling area as the first project. Its gate will be ever locked when not in actual use. That will encourage Debedeavon to be trustworthy, eh?"

"May I consult with my wife before giving you my answer? With our child so soon to be born, she may wish to remain near Jane and her aunt, Jane Pierce, for awhile."

"Of course, of course, but impress upon her the dangers of the impending fevers." He picked up a stack of papers.

"And one thing more, Sir George. Now that military units are forming, I should like to know when I can expect to be called."

"The first unit is already patrolling the area about Jamestown. You should go with the next, which is to destroy nearby villages and drive the Indians to the west and away from our settlements."

"Is this retaliation so necessary? Will it not incite them to further attacks? More of our men are certain to be killed and wounded."

"We have no choice! The Virginia Company and the crown will expect us to take the field in our own defense. They will send us no men, weapons, nor military supplies should we fail to help ourselves promptly, aggressively."

"Then we are to drive the Indians from their ancestral villages and hunting lands with blazing cannons and muskets?"

"Correct. And if you think this plan is heartless, think on the cruel deaths of our neighbors and friends."

"We both lost a dear friend in John Rolfe," said D'Arcy. "I was myself paralyzed with terror that terrible morning as the Indians sped toward my home, my wife. I know the logic of what you say. Yet something within me rebels at these plans for cold-blooded revenge."

"God helps us!" exploded Sir George, his color rising. "Do you think that Wyatt and I find any joy in this course of action? Not only is it our sworn duty, it is essential to safeguard the survivors and to ensure that there will not be another bloody assault. I wake at night in a cold sweat, tortured by the possibility that the Indians may be allied with the Spaniards to the south! Should this actually be the case, we stand in imminent danger of attack by ships! Yes, D'Arcy, a determined and united attack now could mean our defeat—complete and utter defeat!" In his agitation he rose and paced the floor.

"I appreciate your explanation. You have no alternative to taking action against them. When do you want me to report?"

"Next Monday. By the time your three-week stint is over, I expect to have Fortescue moved down here with most of the people from Flowerdieu, their belongings, food supplies, and domestic animals. They will be resettled at Hungar's Creek at the earliest time possible. You will be needed here to help to organize and expedite that venture."

"Some men are to remain at Flowerdieu to safeguard our tobacco crop?"

"Yes, then all the men will return for the harvesting. Come now and walk down the path with me for my meeting at the governor's house. I am putting Councilman Roger Smith in charge of the militia in the Henrico region."

"If only you had been appointed marshal right after Marshal Thomas Neuce died!" said D'Arcy and fell into step.

Military Duty

Becky had been expecting it. She had silently watched the men drilling. Now she and Jane helped D'Arcy pack his gear. "Have you heard that Burgess William Tucker was married this afternoon?"

"No, I had not heard that." D'Arcy looked from Becky to Jane. He knew that she had been watching for Tucker to make a return visit. It seemed a natural enough course of events for the husband's good friend to develop a romantic notion regarding the attractive...and land-rich...widow. And the plight of motherless babes must have seemed a strong attraction to the childless widow. Whatever had gone amiss?

Jane looked pale, but stated with her head high, "I have allowed myself the dreams of a foolish young girl! There had been nothing said, nothing at all. He simply married one who came on the brides' ship *Warwick* last December, and a recent widow."

The evening slipped away all too rapidly. Before light they were breaking their fast. Nobody spoke. The sloop was to sail at dawn. The moment of D'Arcy's departure was here.

"It is just a training time, a bit of patrolling," Becky said as she placed her hands on his shoulders.

"Yes, just training. Nothing to worry about." Then his voice took on the ring of truth, "I'll be back in three weeks." He had no intention of telling her that the men were going out to avenge their relatives and friends.

"Then you will be back before Hopeful is born?"

"Are you sure? I wish I could know that."

"First babies are always slow to arrive. Do you not know even that about them?" She was being gallant about this.

"It is time to go." He kissed her with his arms strong around her.

"Take good care of yourself. Hurry home!" The trite words sounded silly as she spoke them, but how full of meaning! She had never realized how much she loved him, how much she wanted him to stay evermore beside her! Would he live to come back? Was this to be their last moment together in life? "You will miss your boat."

"I wish I would!" He gave her a big smile, one to hold in her heart forever. "Good bye, Jane. I entrust her to you."

"Jane, open the door, and you can help me shove this hero out to do his timely military duty."

That bit of nonsense helped them all through the next few moments of his departure and the repeated farewells.

"This house is certainly quiet without that guardsman," Becky stated, and Jane handed her a handkerchief.

D'Arcy was not planning to offer his services indefinitely to the militia. He could scarcely wait to finish this assignment. He was utterly miserable in body, heart, and soul. He detested military life.

Was there anything worse than this damp cold ground in the early morning? The fog chilled him. Dew sat wetly on everything. His clothes felt wet, lumpy. Now the birds were starting their morning racket! No more sleep today. Might as well get up. Would there be more bloodshed again today?

The food prepared by untrained cooks was terrible. The corn mush was either too salty or too flat, but always full of lumps. There was no milk, as gunshots had frightened off the goat. It was a poor start to a weary day. Becky…how was Becky this morning?

The marching began. They were patrolling a long stretch along the outskirts of the settled lands. The black water swamps caused long detours. The honeysuckle vines caught their ankles and tripped them. Blackberry vines snagged and tore their legs or caught at their hands. Holly trees seemed to lie in wait to torment them with needlelike thorns. Nettles set any exposed part of their legs or arms to itching and burning.

D'Arcy was plodding along, glad of one thing only. There were not enough helmets and breastplates for all of them, so only the regulars wore them. On this hot, muggy morn he was relieved that he did not have to sweat under all that heavy equipment.

Where were the Indians today? He trusted they were far and gone. Nobody relished the idea of more arrows winging silently from a screen of swamp growth.

The gnats hung in clouds. Mosquitoes rose to attack whenever their bushes were disturbed.

"Mr. Southall, would ye look at the beastie in the tree yonder," said Giles quietly just behind him, for they were ordered to make the least possible noise. "Would that be a raccoon now with its black mark...," and his foot veered off the trail, as he turned his head to keep his eye on the animal. He gave a sharp cry of terror.

D'Arcy turned quickly, chilled with instant fear. It was no human enemy but a long, chestnut red and copper-colored snake that was slithering away under the leaves. It must have been four feet long—a huge copperhead! Giles was screaming in panic, but not from pain as yet.

"Giles, lie down!" D'Arcy commanded. "Call the captain down here. Now, Giles, try to calm down. It will be best for you. Hold still! I am tying this vine around your leg; now lie quiet."

The captain came and lost no time in slashing open the snakebite just above the ankle.

D'Arcy moved away. The sudden fright, together with the captain's seemingly ruthless treatment, had made him nauseated. Nor was he the only one. They had been told what was to be done for snakebite, but only the captain had seen this and had treated other cases.

"Carry him to higher ground. We'll have to make camp for a day or so. Can't march with him. Too far to send him back to the fort or on to a plantation. We can't spare the men anyhow." The captain was binding a rag over the wound, easing up gradually on the vine to allow circulation to begin again.

The men moved on until they located a well-fortifiable place with fresh water and dry ground. They spent the rest of the day making rude shelters: the first for Giles, the others for themselves for protection against the burning sun and possible rain. Smoking fires helped to ward off some of the insects.

Would Giles live?

D'Arcy had rarely felt so heavyhearted. The lack of activity gave him time to relive the sickening horror of the snakebite. He dreaded an attack by the Indians, who might see their fire. He was homesick as never before. Would the baby be born while he was away? This was the hardest part of all.

The moaning of the sick youth had them all on edge. Did he have a chance? Adults usually live through a bite from a copperhead. Children up to the teen years cannot tolerate so much poison in their systems. Borderline for this slight fellow. His keening moans penetrated the camp area.

That was the night that a skunk wandered into camp, and of course, one of the men frightened him. Would they ever feel free of that disagreeable odor? Owls hooted. Were these real or Indian signals? A whippoorwill set up its monotonous call.

Try as he would, D'Arcy could not shut out these night sounds and the penetrating smell of the skunk. The shrill, continuous singing of frogs had never seemed so loud and insistent. To think that he and Becky had agreed that the sound was pleasant, even musical. Oh, Becky! Would morning ever come?

A grey dawn found the men hollow eyed and grumpy from lack of rest, but Giles was better. He would live. They would stay in camp for two more days with patrols going out. A hunting party was being formed, and D'Arcy volunteered.

That evening he took the hide of the deer they had shot and began tanning it to have something to occupy himself.

First he mixed cornmeal with birds' eggs and rubbed that into the undersurface of the skin. He stretched it on a twig frame. After it dried, he placed it over a smoky fire for an hour to preserve its softness, even if it should get wet.

So the time went by and each day left scars on his memory. At last the final village was burned with the terrified Indians escaping, racing off with only what they could clutch in their hands of their life's necessities. Training his musket on them, driving them to the north and west, D'Arcy jerked up his aim, and the shot went over their heads.

What if this village were Chanco's!

Soon after that the unit returned to Jamestown. He rushed from the sloop to the Rolfe house. "Becky!" He called at the door.

"Oh, D'Arcy, at last you are home!" and she was in his arms. "You soldiers are men of overwhelming powers, a few I can name: smoke, sweat, gunpowder, leather, and can that be skunk?"

"I got here before Hopeful!" He laughed a little unsteadily. "If you knew how I missed you…skunk? It came into camp weeks ago."

"And I missed you. Today I feel so trembling and strange that I think we shall not have to wait much longer. Let's take a little walk."

"I have a present for you: a deerskin that I tanned myself, Indian style. It turned out to be very soft and fine, but I warn you, it does smell…smoky!"

Hopeful

And so it was that D'Arcy came home on the lovely day in early May when Becky, aided by her aunt and cousin, had her child.

D'Arcy had hours and hours at his disposal to bathe and dress in clean clothes at long last, to enjoy the well-prepared meal that Jane's cook served him, and to stroll about the well-tended grounds that had been John Rolfe's pride.

He was feeling human again and very excited when Jane called to him, "She is ready to see you now."

"What is it, a boy or girl?"

"She will tell you. I am not going to deny her that pleasure!"

"You are tormenting me."

Becky thought she had never seen him look so handsome as when he entered the room. "D'Arcy, look here."

He looked down at the pink little infant, all wrapped in a blanket. He picked up his child and held it close. It felt so light and soft. It smelled so sweet. "Hopeful…at last! That was a long wait you put us through. What a fine looking baby we have, Becky, my dear. Thank you." Placing the baby by her side, he kissed her long and tenderly.

"You do not seem to care whether we have a son or daughter."

"I do care!"

"We have a son, D'Arcy."

"I could not be happier. Yet a little girl would please me as much. Does this make sense to you?"

"What shall we name him? What do you suggest?"

"You say it first, Becky."

"John."

"I too was going to suggest John. He must bear the name of our friend, John Rolfe."

"Do call Jane and my dear aunt. I want them to know."

In this way Jane learned that the little boy she had helped to bring into the world was named for her late husband. She stood by the wind hole, looking out over the broad river, and her eyes were full of tears. She felt joy that the baby had arrived safely, grief for her dead husband and her own childless widowhood, but comfort in the news that the boy would all his life carry the name of John Rolfe.

Cousin Jane

Not long after this it so happened that Councilman Roger Smith sailed down the James from Henrico, where he had charge of the militia, and stopped at Jamestown. He was paying for fruit trees that he was ordering from Sir George, as the nursery stock was being rapidly depleted despite the current crisis. These trees were not for his home in Jamestown, but for some land on the south side of the river. It was land to which he did not as yet have title, as it had been patented by John Rolfe.

One day this land would be famous for its Smithfield hams, but now he was arriving in Jamestown to meet Yeardley and conclude their business regarding the date of delivery. Then they came together to pay their respects to Jane Rolfe, widow of their late colleague on the council.

Smith must have sent Jane a message by some secret sign, for presently they quietly drifted away for a stroll by the river.

"Now that," chuckled Sir George, "explains Smith's coming here today." And he winked at Becky.

"What do you know of this man!" asked D'Arcy. "All that I can recall is that he arrived in Virginia about a year after I did, and by the next he had charmed his way onto the council."

"As a provisional councilor please note, D'Arcy. We were not at all sure that he would work out. He is a very dynamic sort—aggressive, but a surprisingly able member of the group as it soon developed. This is why he has recently been given the title of full councilman, as well as captain in the militia—born administrator."

"Or a born opportunist? I wonder if I am jealous of this man?" mused D'Arcy. "Here he comes, storming into our midst, and within two years' time he is making decisions that determine what happens in all of our lives. What does he actually know of the people here?"

"If you were just arriving, whose career would you choose to follow: his or yours? Which way of life would give the greater satisfaction?" asked Becky.

"The answer to your wife's question should be very interesting," murmured Sir George, lighting his pipe and then slipping his finger into John's strong little fist.

"You are asking," replied D'Arcy, "if I actually benefited from the experiences of sitting in the stocks; lugging bricks; hunting and fishing for the communal meals; collecting naval stores; writing letters for the illiterate; listening to the men spinning yarns over their ale; taking my turn as needed at military duties; knowing you and John Rolfe as friends, rather than as committeemen to outwit across the council table; trading with the Indians; attending the first meeting of the House of Burgesses; planting tobacco; meeting those Indians face to face in the massacre; even surviving a near-fatal illness. But I feel that my most worthwhile work has been instructing the children.

"Looking back," he continued, "I am glad I had a part in the daily work that causes Jamestown to grow and prosper. I feel that I know these people. Looking ahead, Becky and I have begun our family," and his eyes rested proudly on John before they lifted to Becky's.

"Well said," commented Sir George. "I had not heard of some of these experiences of yours. Well, here come our friends."

One look at Jane's face told them there would be glad news. "Roger has asked me to be his wife," and Jane smiled up at the handsome man at her side.

Becky wordlessly gave her an embrace. Her heart was too full to speak. Jane would again love and be loved. Her loneliness was coming to an end.

The room was full of hearty congratulations and laughter. John began to cry. Becky picked him up from his cradle and patted his back gently. "We were about to plan the christening, and Jane is to be godmother."

"Will you be John's godfather, Captain Smith?" asked D'Arcy.

"Only on the condition that I be addressed as Roger by the members of my dear Jane's family," replied Roger Smith with a broad smile, and D'Arcy had to admit to himself that the man had a most pleasant and friendly personality. Who besides Becky noticed that Roger had finished buying the fruit trees for the Rolfe land before Jane agreed to marry him?

Eastern Shore

It was June 1623. Marshal George Yeardley was making a final stop on his inspection tour of the defenses that he had planned and established in the previous three months throughout the Chesapeake Bay area and the James River valley. His sloop moved into the anchorage at Hungar's Creek, and the sails were lowered. The marshal came ashore attended by a group that included the Reverend Bolton, who was bringing religious comfort not only to Yeardley's people but also to those of Lady Elizabeth Dale, who had settled nearby.

Sergeant Fortescue led the people in their holiday mood and dress to welcome their master to his new plantation. Already the community looked well established to Yeardley's well-trained eye, and he eagerly anticipated inspecting the stout palisade that surrounded the village. The people looked happy and, to his enormous relief, in the best of health.

Sir George sighed. "Here you have been free of the foul distemper that has cost the lives of so many along the James. We think perhaps the epidemic was brought in by the refugees."

"In this and in other ways we have been blessed with good fortune," replied Sergeant Fortescue as D'Arcy and Becky came forward to pay their respects.

"How are Lady Temperance and the children?" worriedly inquired Becky.

"They are well, praise God, especially with our new infant expected in December. The location of our home on Back River, apart from the crowded areas, may have saved us from illness and grief."

"We are very grateful to you, Sir George," D'Arcy greeted his friend and benefactor, "for making this place available to us. Life here is most pleasant. We are at peace with Chief Debedeavon and his Accomacks, with whom we carry on a most lively trade."

"So your early try to barter with them has been of some use to you, eh? You are tutoring the children?"

"Yes, and training Jamie to do likewise. I hope soon to hear that a school in Jamestown will be available to the children like Dickin's."

But the look that crossed Yeardley's face told him that Dickin's little ones were now beyond their reach. "Dickin himself still lives, but the rest of his family...the fever. He has sent you some ale and his compliments."

D'Arcy could not speak.

Sir George took John from Becky and held the thriving infant. He smiled as he tickled the top of the little head with the tip of his trim, pointed beard.

Becky broke the silence. "Sir George, since the massacre you have labored to the point of exhaustion to strengthen defenses and to restore a sense of security to the colony. Here you will find peace, which you yourself have made possible. Stay here with us for a time. Enjoy the new life."

"With those transplanted from Flowerdieu," finished D'Arcy.

Sir George's roar of laughter was what had been missing at Hungar's Creek. "I suppose I could spare some time to ease off for a while. A house for my use has been prepared, you say, Fortescue? Pray send to Jamestown for my wife and children to join me for...say six weeks. Now let us be off to see what you have done in the way of construction here about."

"Perhaps you would also like to change into your country clothing, Sir George, and join Jamie and me for a bit of duck hunting before the feast?" suggested D'Arcy.

"This is promising to be a very welcome respite, indeed it is," and with a final tickle with his Van Dyke beard, he returned John to D'Arcy. "Reverend Bolton and Fortescue," he continued, "I urge you to join us to hunt these excellent ducks of Hungar's Creek."

"We need your eagle eyes," added D'Arcy, "to bring in enough for a roast duck dinner at eventide tomorrow. The best time to approach the marshes now draws near. Let us ready ourselves to take the trail!"

With a loving smile, D'Arcy placed in Becky's waiting arms their son and stake in the future.

Primary Sources of Reference

Abernathy, Thomas, Perkins. Introduction. *Notes on the State of Virginia* by Thomas Jefferson. New York: Harper and Row, 1964.

Complete Works of Shakespeare, with temple notes. Word Syndicate Publishing Co. Cleveland, Ohio, New York, NY (no author or date) 1930s. *As You Like It.* 2.7.9.1-2, 2.7.9.2-3. *Macbeth* 5.5.5.8-10.

Dowdey, Clifford. *The Great Plantation*. New York: Bonanza Books, 1957.

Southall, Donna Doe. *Indians of Virginia in the Seventeenth Century.*Term Paper, University of Virginia,1964. (Revised 1967)

Swem, E.G. (Ed.) (1957). *Jamestown 350th Anniversary Historical Booklets.* Williamsburg: Virginia 350th Anniversary Celebration Corporation. (23 booklets)

Truman, Nora Miller. *George Yeardley: Governor of Virginia.* Richmond: Garrett and Massie Inc., 1959.